Mr. Zip
and
The Capital Z

Kimberly Bryant-Palmer

Illustrated by Jerry Palmer

Mr. Zip and The Capital Z

Library of Congress Control Number: 2015909380

ISBN Print: 978-0-9962546-0-1
ISBN eBook: 978-0-9962546-1-8
ISBN ePDF: 978-0-9962546-2-5

Mr. Zip and The Capital Z may be purchased at special quantity discounts. Resale opportunities are
available for churches, donor programs, fund raising, book clubs, or educational purposes for churches, congregations,
schools and universities. For more information contact Kimberly: Kimberly@mrzipbooks.com.

Have Kimberly Palmer and/or Jerry Palmer speak at your church, fundraiser or special event.
For information email Kimberly@mrzipbooks.com.

1. Restoration 2. History 3. Imagination 4. Family 5. Trust   6. Loyalty 7. Decisions 8. Journey
I. Bryant-Palmer, Kimberly: Palmer, Jerry II. Mr. Zip and The Capital Z

Author: Kimberly Bryant-Palmer
Illustrated by Jerry Palmer
Edited by Anne Severance
Cover and Interior Design by Jared Rowe
Original layout by Don Wise
Publishing Consultant: Mel Cohen of Inspired Authors Press
Website: www.mrzipbooks.com

Kimberly Bryant-Palmer
P.O. Box 680085
Franklin, TN 37068
Kimberly@mrzipbooks.com

To my mom, Martha Toy Walls,
who took me to the library every week
and taught me to choose a book by its well-worn cover.

To my daddy, Ray Allen Strange,
who once, as a young boy, had a crush on a little girl...
She was "as sweet as honey, but the bees didn't know it!"

To my children—John, Laura, and Daniel—
each one so different, but each, a delight!

To my dear, sweet husband, Jerry,
who gave me the idea for this book…and his love.
~ Kimberly

and

To Esther Niles, my high school history teacher,
Wellston High School, St. Louis, MO, 1965,
who taught me to love America and American history…passionately.
Thank you, "Lady Esther."
~ Jerry

CONTENTS

Introducing the Johnson Family
or, better yet…
What it Means to Be a Johnson

When Peanut Johnson of the East Side Johnsons made his initial appearance into this world, he was one of the cutest babies ever to grace the sweet valley where his family lived. Surrounded by aunts and the town's midwife, Peanut Johnson of the lower East Side Johnsons opened the most sincerely polite, biggest brown eyes when seeing his world for the first time. Everyone was smiling down at him, but it wasn't until the midwife took him out to meet his daddy that Peanut Johnson's big brown eyes took on a twinkle so deep his dad broke into a grin. "Why, son, look at you. You are as cute as a little peanut." And *that* is how "Peanut" Johnson got his name, his real name.

Now, you might think that is a strange way to get your name, but it would only be because you had never met the Johnson family. Every Johnson's name tells its own story.

"Early" Johnson, Peanut's dad, got his name because

he was born very early in the morning on January 1. On the day he was born, Early's dad, who wanted to sleep a little longer than midnight, was mildly disgruntled with this all-too-early arrival. As he climbed up into the rickety wagon to go get the midwife, he decided in mumbled yawns he would name that baby Early, and that's just what he did!

Counting Peanut, there are seven children in the Johnson family. The oldest, "Secret," is 19 years old. She got her name because the Johnsons, wanting to surprise everyone, kept the secret of her coming as long as they could. She has grown into a beautiful woman, quite like her mama. She sings all the time and when she walks into a room, well, that room…it just lights up.

"Big Baby," the oldest son, weighed 12 pounds when he was born. The midwife, not knowing the Johnson tradition, said he should be named Goliath, which would have been better for him as he grew, since it is difficult for a boy to wear the name Big Baby with honor. That no longer seems to matter since he is almost 6'7", weighs over 300 pounds, and is still growing at 18. Some may want to tease him about his name, but with the first "Hey, Big Baby," those who know him dive for cover, and those who don't, wish they had. His mama dotes on him, and he carries her 4'10" cuteness around when he comes home, to the squeals of the other kids and her laughing and saying, "Baby, put me down." Even though Big Baby growls when people tease him about his name, he is the most gentle of the Johnsons with a heart that is as loving and tender as he is big.

"Pocket" is the next boy. Unlike Big Baby, Pocket came early and weighed only 2 ½ pounds. "Why, he is so small, he could fit in my pocket," said Early and thus came his name. Pocket, small for being 16, is smart and helps his dad with the figures at the mill where he works. Pocket wears a button-down shirt and tie everyday, the tie seeming too long because Pocket is so short. Pocket reads and studies all the time and knows the answers to most questions, especially ones from Big Baby, who always seems to have a lot of them. You will hardly ever see Pocket without Big Baby. If they were not two years apart, you might think they were fraternal twins. Not surprisingly, no one picks on Pocket, because with Pocket comes Big Baby!

"Royal" is next in line. When he was born, his skin tone was a beautiful black—so black, in fact, that in the right light, it takes on a purplish hue. Since his skin is the purplish color kings wear, Royal fancies himself as a rather princely fellow and, therefore, dresses as a prince should. His shirts are always pressed and his ties, perfect. He never seems to perspire, no matter how much work he does, what kind of work, or how hot the day is. Even if he is working in the mud, he somehow manages to keep himself clean. A fact that is a true marvel!

Next is "Whisper." When Mrs. Johnson (her first name is Katherine, but everyone calls her Kat) told Early she was to have another baby, she took him for a walk in the park by the little waterfall fountain and whispered very softly in his ear, "You will soon be a daddy again." Early smiled so big and kissed Kat and smiled some more. When the new baby was born, he named her Whisper because Kat had whispered the news to him. Whisper fits her name. She talks softly and smiles all the time. She loves everybody, finds the good in everything, never raises her voice, and prays with each breath.

Peanut is next and, for a long time following, there were no newborn babies in the Johnson household. Kat and Early gave the crib and hand-me-down clothes to Marvin and Inez Crumbler, a young married couple who were expecting their first baby. When they wagged their baby stuff over to the Crumblers, Kat and Early watched the tears of gratitude flow down Inez's face. Grateful and happy they had helped someone in need, they returned home only to find a few months later, they probably should have waited!

Once again, Kat took Early on the peaceful walk to the little waterfall fountain, and after giving him a nice kiss and he giving her one back, told him they were going to have another baby. Since Kat had given Early such a nice kiss when she told him the news, he decided to name the baby "Lovie Dovie."

And that is how the children of the Johnson family got their names. All of them were admired, respected, and liked by everyone, especially Peanut.

Now, everyone *loved* Peanut Johnson. No one could ever remember an unkind word he had ever spoken or an unkind deed he had ever done. And his eyes, oh my, his deeply brown, sincerely polite, merry, and sometimes mischievous eyes made anyone his friend, kids and grown-ups alike. He was the friend who would always have fun with you. He was the friend you could trust to be mischievous with you, the friend to be afraid with you, and even the friend to be sad with you. He was your best friend. He was *everyone's* best friend. And even though everyone knew Peanut Johnson was everyone else's best friend, *that* was okay because everyone knew that they and all their adventures were safe with him.

But it was not *always* that way. Oh, no! The wise young man behind Peanut Johnson's deeply brown, sincerely polite, merry, mischievous eyes had to learn a lesson that made his heart ache…one day, not so long ago.

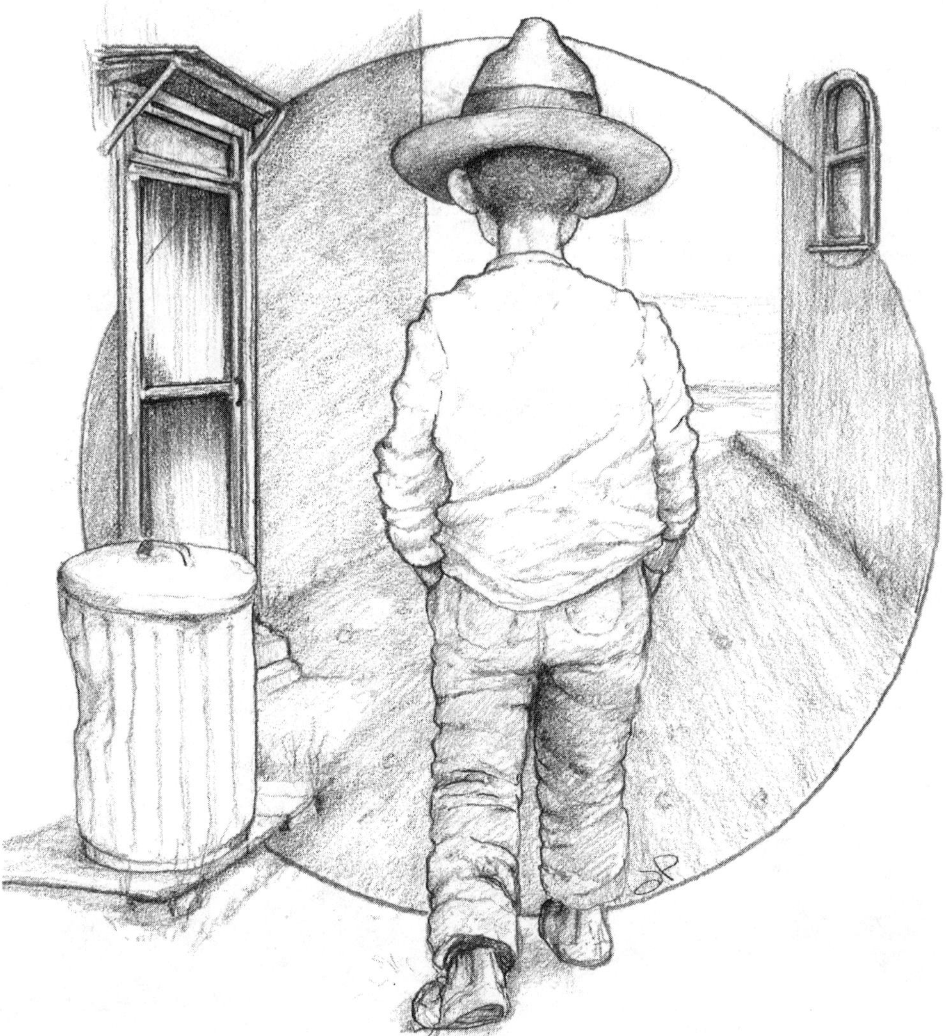

Chapter 1

This, That, and Uncle Milkweed, Too!

Peanut Johnson walked slowly down the alley that dusty July day. His head hung so low that his hat, a felt fedora that was already too big and much too hot to wear in July, fell forward on his face, almost completely covering his sincerely polite, big brown eyes. Kicking a stone, the what-happened-the-day-before-yesterday replay swirled in his mind like the dusty clouds of dirt that swirled around his feet as he walked aimlessly along.

The town had settled back into the lazy, hot quiet that happens the day after the Fourth of July. Parades and parties, pie cook-offs, and all the excited people had melted back into the everyday summertime life of a small town. Most shops had remained closed for the holiday weekend, so Peanut Johnson really did not have anywhere to go or much of anything to do. Not really wanting to see anyone he knew, Peanut Johnson was quite okay kicking that particular stone down that dusty alleyway on that particular day. That is… until he reached the corner of the alleyway and Main Street, across from the First Pedestrian Church (yes, that's really its name, but that's a story for later).

Hanging like an old-time medical shingle above arched oak doors was a sign that read: "The Capital Z—a This and That Shop." Unlike all the shops and stores that were closed, with blinds pulled down and lights now dark, the lights of The Capital Z were warm and friendly, and the blinds of The Capital Z were raised in an invitation that said, "Come on in!"

Timidly peeking through the glass portion of the arched doors, Peanut Johnson saw just what the sign said, and even more. There were trinkets and other smaller items carefully displayed on countertops and shelves, but it seemed to Peanut, looking from the outside in, that there were more

things inside than he or *anyone* could ever think about, or want. Why, there was even a canoe, a cannon, and, if you could believe it, a large bale of cotton! Peanut raised one eyebrow somewhat skeptically.

Looking around a little more, he spotted a gentleman perched on a stool at a desk in the middle of the shop. He was a wiry-looking fellow, older, too—*real* old, but Peanut couldn't say *that!* He couldn't call him "an old man," not even in his thoughts, because that would be disrespectful. Shaking his head, Peanut *did* allow himself to think that the older gentleman had to be *at least* 50 years old!

He also seemed to be tall, because Peanut could see that even with his feet resting on the bottom rung of the stool, his bony legs (which Peanut could see because the man was wearing old-style knickers) barely fit under a desk that was at least 3½ feet high. His glasses, which looked more like ole-time spectacles, rested on the tip of a somewhat ski-sloped nose. He really was an odd-looking gentleman, but Peanut couldn't help feeling that this wiry, older man had a kindness about him and that he was really okay.

Peanut hesitated, lingering a little longer outside the doors of The Capital Z, and watched him closely. The gentleman was studying something and seemed to be deep in thought, so deep, Peanut Johnson hoped—*really* hard—that he could *probably* sneak in without being noticed. Removing his hat (because that is a gentlemanly thing to do) and pushing the doors open ever so carefully and ever so quietly (because, remember, he really did not want to see or talk to anyone that particular hot day after the Fourth of July), he took his first step into The Capital Z. He had almost succeeded in sneaking in when those old, arched, saloon-like doors brushed past tinkling bells.

Peanut stopped where he was, his face wrinkling as he shut his eyes tight in exasperation. In his mind, those tinkling bells had just announced to the world, to everyone, just exactly where he was. The old gentleman sitting atop that high stool looked up and greeted Peanut Johnson with a grin that spread from ear to ear and with twinkling, welcoming eyes that were as warm and friendly as the lights of The Capital Z.

"Why, hello, and welcome to The Capital Z. I'm Aloysius Zip, but you can call me Mr. Zip. And I believe your name is, ummm…"—Mr. Zip paused, putting his finger to the side of his forehead— "let me see…oh, yes…you're Peanut Johnson."

Peanut let out a little gasp. Mr. Zip knew his name? Peanut Johnson stood rooted to the spot. His mouth was frozen half open, and his eyebrows, well, his eyebrows were arched in such surprise, they almost became part of his hairline.

"Come on into The Capital Z! Make yourself at home. If you have any questions, please feel free to ask me anything, anything at all."

Not knowing if he could really ask the question that had just popped into his head, Peanut Johnson cleared his throat. "Ummm...Mr. Zip, why is it called 'The Capital Z'?"

Mr. Zip chuckled. "Well...my name is Aloysius Zip and the shop is a lot like me. Aloysius – A...Zip – Z. Understand? In this shop, there is a little of this and a little of that, everything you would need to know – from A to Z! A capital idea, don't you think?"

"Uhh...okay...I think I see." With that, Peanut took another step into The Capital Z.

Even though you would expect this to be a regular shop with four regular walls, the inside was circular and the ceilings, *incredibly* high. The old wooden floor creaked in greeting as Peanut walked in. To the right was a beautiful spiral staircase with a worn, but shiny wooden railing. Peanut rubbed his hand across the railing and, all of a sudden, it was as if he could *hear* the light-hearted laughter of children and *see* them running happily up and down the stairs. Peanut shook his head, tightly shutting his eyes. When he dared to open one eye, only the old wooden stairs and shiny railing remained. *What was that?* he wondered. He looked over at Mr. Zip, but he didn't ask the question out loud. In fact, he didn't say a word.

Mr. Zip had turned to bend over his desk and was studying something intently. Without looking up, he said, "People tell me that when they're in this shop, they feel like they see or hear unusual things. Sometimes, both."

Under his breath, Peanut muttered, "This place is haunted? Maybe I should leave!" He was about to do just that, but there was so *much*, there were so *many* things to see in The This and That Shop, he *had* to stay! Besides the cannon,

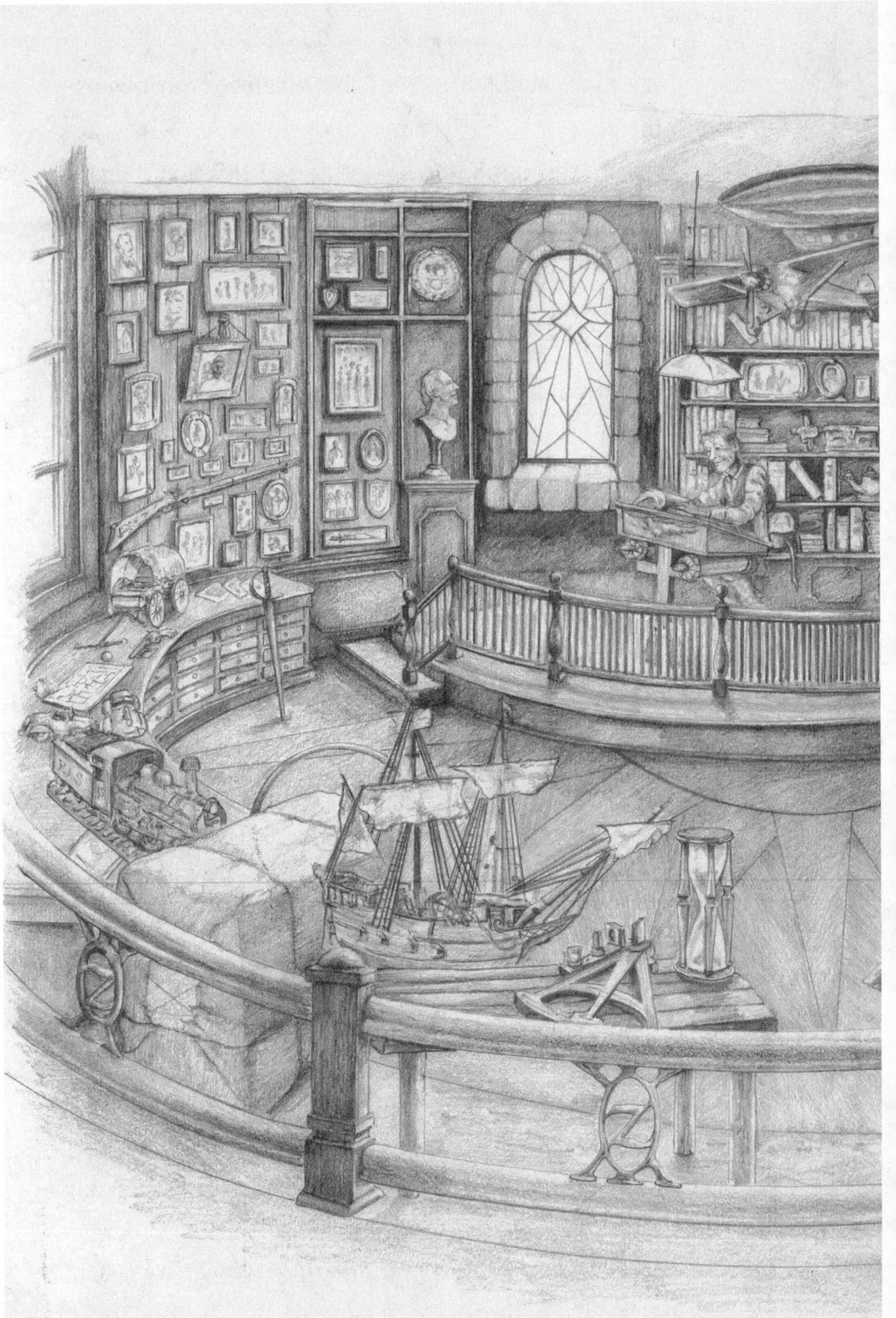

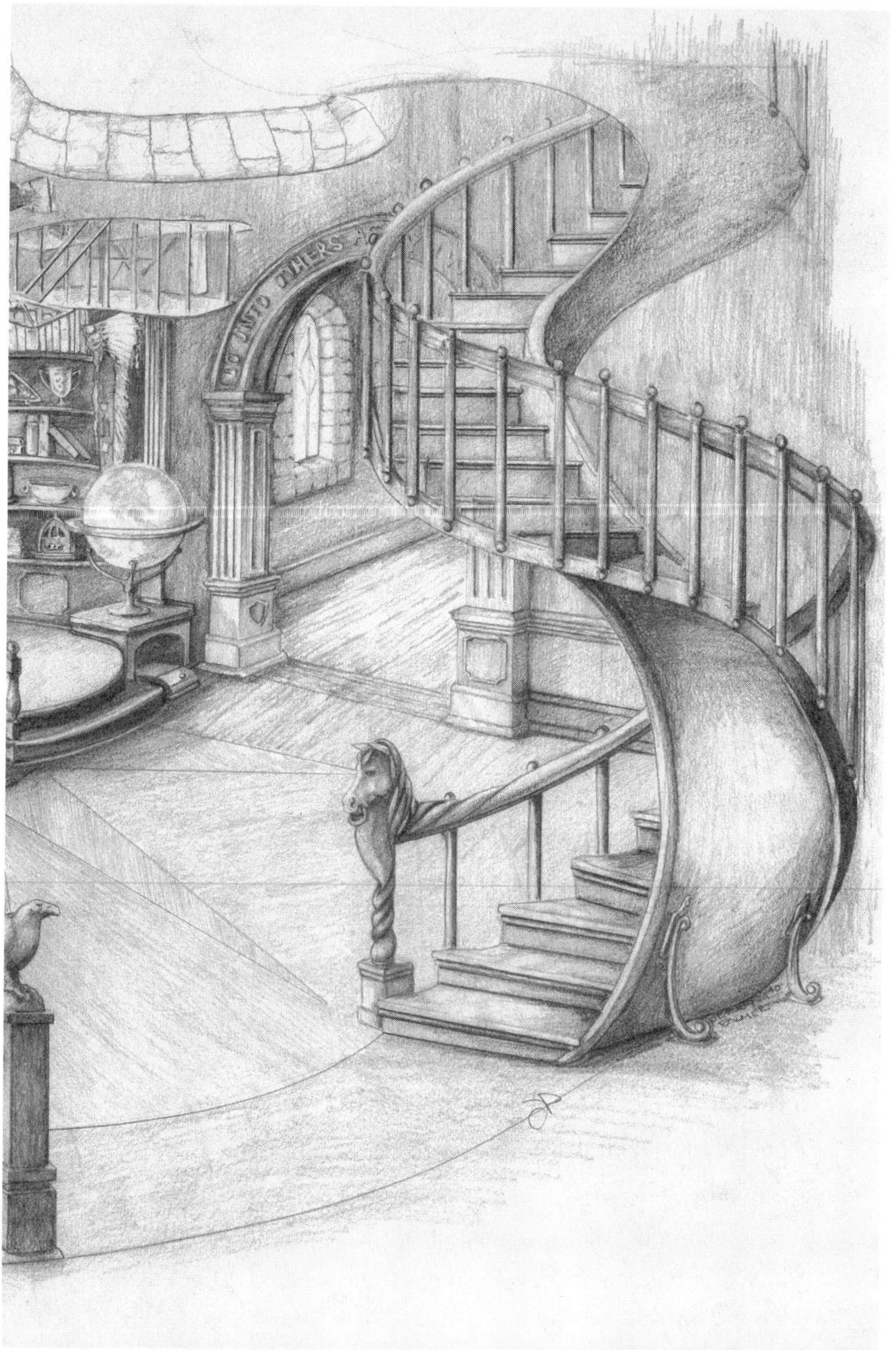
UNTO OTHERS

the canoe, and the bale of cotton Peanut had seen when he was peeking through the window, there were model trains and cars, hula-hoops, and really old-looking, wind-up toys. There were model ships, globes, old radios, statues, puzzles, swords, BB guns, and a miniature wagon that looked so real that, at any moment, Peanut half-expected to see miniature people walking around it. Why, hanging from the ceiling was even a model airplane. If it weren't so small, Peanut thought it looked like it could have been the same plane that the Wright brothers flew at Kitty Hawk, North Carolina.

What Peanut noticed next were photographs, all kinds of photographs—at least 50 of them. There were photos of kids and adults, presidents and other famous people. Judging from what some of them were wearing, Peanut thought some of the photos looked really old, like 100 years old, and some looked almost brand-new as if they were taken yesterday. The really strange thing was that Mr. Zip was in ALL of the photos! Peanut thought that was weird, almost scary, but since everyone was smiling and laughing in the photos, he decided that this place was okay. *There are too many fun things here, and this place just feels too friendly to be haunted.*

Peanut shrugged and took a step when the floor let out an awful "Creeeeeaaaaak" and then another "Creeeeeaaaaak" as he tried to take a second step. "Aw, man!" he said under his breath.

Then he shot a glance at Mr. Zip, who didn't seem to have noticed anything. Peanut let out a sigh of relief and decided to try again. "Creeaak, Creeaak." That old wooden floor was not *about* to let him go unnoticed. It just *wanted* to announce where he was and what he was doing. Peanut was about to give up and leave when, out of the corner of his eye, he saw the most beautiful thing he had ever seen—a rifle! It wasn't just any rifle, either. It looked like it might be a Kentucky rifle! He walked over to investigate.

He was leaning over to take a closer look and was about to sneak a touch (because he didn't know if that was allowed) when Mr. Zip broke the silence. "Feel free to look around or even pick up anything you like."

Peanut nearly jumped out of his skin. Unnerved, he half-mumbled, "Thank you, thank you, Mr. Zip." Moving forward slowly, he was just about to touch the gun when he suddenly remembered the staircase and jerked his hand back. *Wait a minute! What if I do touch it and something happens?* He hesitated just a little more, but that gun was sooo beautiful....

With trembling fingers, he reached out toward the butt of the rifle, then ran his hand its full length. "Wow!" Peanut said, right out loud. "This thing is huge! It must be about six feet long!"

Chuckling, Mr. Zip walked over to Peanut. "Yep, it is huge. Do you know what kind of rifle it is?"

Peanut was beginning to feel at home in The Capital Z. "Yessir, Mr. Zip, I believe I do. It's a Kentucky rifle, isn't it? Looks like a picture my fifth-grade teacher, Mrs. Pendergrass, showed us."

"You're right! This is one of the best, made around 1790 by Christian Hawken in Maryland. Know who was famous for using this rifle?"

"Sure do, Mr. Zip. Andrew Jackson used these rifles to defeat the British in the War of 1812. Mrs. Pendergrass told us that, too. She also taught us a song called 'Hunters of Kentucky.'[1] My sister, Secret, who had Mrs. Pendergrass before I did, used to sing it all the time, so when I got to the fifth grade, I already knew that song. Yessir, uh huh, I did."

Peanut began to hum the tune and, as he did, he began to see in his imagination the riflemen, crouching in the bushes with only the barrels of their rifles peeking through the leaves. He could see them taking aim, then firing, hitting their targets 250 to 500 yards away! *Well, at least that's what Mrs. Pendergrass said,* Peanut thought to himself, shaking his head in amazement.

"You know, we almost lost that one." Mr. Zip's voice brought Peanut back from crouching in the bushes with the Kentucky riflemen.

"What? Uh...*sir?*" Peanut corrected himself.

"We almost lost that war, the one you're humming about. You know, the War of 1812. You might be interested to know that this very rifle was part of that battle. Look at the nameplate, Peanut."

As Peanut looked closely at the well-worn, brass nameplate that was fixed onto the side of the rifle's maple stock, Mr. Zip read aloud:

*This Kentucky Rifle was used by Milkweed
Johnson during The War of 1812 defending
Chalmette, LA, and New Orleans, LA, from those
murderous Redcoats.
Donated in the year of our Lord 1830.*

"Peanut," Mr. Zip asked, "do you know who Milkweed Johnson was and what he did during the War of 1812?"

Peanut shook his head in a polite no.

"Milkweed Johnson was your great-great-great-great-uncle. He was a dark-skinned American, just like you. Born into slavery on the de Trépagnier (d a y - t r a y - p a n - y a y) Plantation just outside New Orleans, Louisiana, Milkweed grew up there. He married a sweet girl named Louisa, and they had three children. Milkweed's owner was Pierre de Trépagnier. The de Trépagnier family lived quite happily several years on their plantation"—Mr. Zip leaned closer and dropped his voice—"but what happened one night is a mystery that has never been solved." "What happened?" Peanut whispered excitedly, as people do when they talk about any mystery, let alone an *unsolved* mystery.

"Well," said Mr. Zip, his eyebrows raised and his eyes twinkling, "in 1796, one night while the de Trépagnier family was having dinner, there was a knock at the door. The house slave who answered the door let in a mysterious visitor and went to get Pierre. When Pierre saw who it was, he grabbed his coat and hat and left in the night with the visitor…and…was…never…seen…again."

"Oh, my!" came the softest exclamation from behind Peanut and Mr. Zip.

Startled, Mr. Zip and Peanut whirled around to find Peanut's sister, Whisper, standing there.

Embarrassed and a little exasperated, Peanut sputtered, "Whisssssper, how did you find me and HOW did you come in without me hearing you, without the bells ringing when the doors open? You just about scared me to death!"

Whisper, smiling softly, shrugged her shoulders. "I don't know, I just slipped in. Besides, I was as loud as an elephant." And then, once again, in a placating tone, "I followed you here, Peanut. I just wanted to make sure you were okay."

When he heard her concern, Peanut's defenses dropped a little, along with his shoulders. "Oh, Whisper, I'm fine. I'm okay."

Peanut was just turning to introduce Whisper to Mr. Zip, when Mr. Zip jumped in, extending his hand. "Hello there, Whisper, I'm Mr. Zip. Welcome to The Capital Z."

Whisper, being the gentle soul that she was, smiled sweetly and nodding hello, shook just one of Mr. Zip's fingers. "My, this is a lovely shop you have, Mr. Zip, lovely and HUGE. I mean, I mean," Whisper stammered just a little, "I mean no offense, Mr. Zip, it's just that I would have never imagined so many things in this seemingly small building!" Whisper continued, craning her neck to look ALL around.

Mr. Zip laughed heartily. "Yes, it is a pretty big shop. There are a lot of things in The Capital Z. Would you like for me to show you around?"

And then, as if suddenly remembering something, Whisper said, "Oh no, thank you, Mr. Zip. I need to get back home. Mama and I are going to bake some cookies today. I just wanted to see Peanut."

"Whisper, don't you want to know what happened to the de Trépagnier family?" Peanut asked.

"I do, but I need to go."

"But you're gonna miss out and it's just getting really good!" Peanut said, trying a little harder to convince her to stay.

"Will you tell me later?"

"You know I will."

"Well, you must come back another day," said Mr. Zip.

"I will, I will, I promise." Whisper turned to leave.

"Wait a second, Whisper," Peanut said. "I'll walk you to the door."

And with that, Peanut and Whisper headed for the front of The Capital Z, bumping into each other affectionately on the way. As Whisper was leaving, she turned and, gently touching Peanut on the shoulder, walked out the swinging doors.

…that mountain men used the Hawken rifle to
kill bear and buffalo?

Chapter 2

Peanut Johnson Sticks with It

After the old oak doors gently ushered Whisper out of The Capital Z, Peanut bounded back to Mr. Zip and planted himself right where he had been before. "Okay, Mr. Zip, what happened next? What happened when Pierre left with the mysterious visitor?"

"To this day, no one knows, Peanut. Mrs. de Trépagnier held onto the plantation as long as she could, about two years, then sold it to a Mr. Butler, an Irishman. He renamed his new home the 'Ormond Plantation' after a castle in Ireland." Mr. Zip paused, recollecting the facts, then added, "Mr. Butler was known far and wide for being a fair and decent man."

Peanut frowned. "But wait a minute, Mr. Zip. I'm a little confused. What does this have to do with my Great-Great-Great-Great-Uncle Milkweed?"

"In 1792, when the de Trépagniers still owned the plantation, Milkweed ran away to Kentucky and settled in a little town called Elizabethton. He did not feel good about running away because he had always tried to do what was right. Also, he was worried about the family he had left behind. In fact, it weighed so heavily on his heart, it almost crushed him."

Peanut looked down, shuffling his feet, as if what Mr. Zip had just said made him somewhat nervous. Mr. Zip wondered why, but Peanut was listening so intently, he decided to continue. "Your Great-Great-Great-Great-Uncle—how about we just call him Uncle Milkweed—had heard from other escaped slaves that Master de Trépagnier had vanished and that the plantation had a new owner. In spite of the possible danger of being recaptured, especially by the new owner, Milkweed was still determined to go back and buy his freedom…to get papers stating that he was a freed man…and one day, buy his family's freedom, too.

"So your Uncle Milkweed began to work any job he could find. He scraped and saved everything he earned, except for just enough to get by. He often worked many jobs at the same time, but one job, that to you and me might almost seem silly, became the most important thing Milkweed ever did. Why, that job actually changed his life!"

"What was it, Mr. Zip?" Peanut asked, now thoroughly caught up in the story of his uncle.

"Weelll, Milkweed helped some farmers in Kentucky by shooting groundhogs, chipmunks, and really, any pesky critters that destroyed crops. And you know, Peanut, he became quite good at it, too!"

"WHAT?" Peanut could hardly believe his ears. "Aw, Mr. Zip, you're teasing me. How could shooting chipmunks or groundhogs or any of those other animals change anyone's life?"

"Well, Peanut, how big would you say a chipmunk might be?"

Peanut held his hands about four inches apart. "Maybe about this big, Mr. Zip, maybe a little bigger."

"And a groundhog?"

"Well, a groundhog is much bigger than a chipmunk, Mr. Zip. It's about the size of a cat. Anyone knows that."

"Yes, but both of those animals are really quick. Right, Peanut?"

"Yessir, you're right. But, Mr. Zip, I don't get it. What does shooting groundhogs, chipmunks, and squirrels have to do with changing my Great-Great-Great-Great... oops...I mean, my Uncle Milkweed's life?"

"Peanut, are you really good at something— something that makes folks think of you whenever that something is mentioned?"

"Yessir, Mr. Zip," said Peanut, puffing his chest out just a little, but also bashfully shuffling his feet, because for sure and for certain, he did not want to be a braggart. "I can really hit a baseball out of the park."

At that very moment, the oak doors of The Capital Z burst open with decided gusto, as if they were announcing somebody. Indeed they were, for who should walk in but Big Baby and Pocket.

Without waiting for any kind of introduction, Big Baby, with the kindest eyes and the warmest, deepest drawl, said, "Ho, Peanut, Whisper said we could find you here.

How're ya doin', little fella?"

Pocket, who always spoke rapidly and precisely, interrupted, "He's fine, Big Baby. Anyone can see that." He turned to Peanut. "You're fine, Peanut, right? You're fine?" Suddenly seeing Mr. Zip for the first time, Pocket shot out his hand to shake Mr. Zip's. "Hello, I'm Pocket Johnson, and you are…"

Extending his hand, Mr. Zip replied, "Aloysius Zip, at your service, but everyone calls me Mr. Zip. Welcome to The Capital Z."

"What are you guys doin'?" Big Baby asked, cutting in, but in such a sweet and caring way, no one minded.

"As a matter of fact, your brother was just telling me about how he can hit a baseball out of the park," Mr. Zip replied.

"Oh, yessir, yessir, that's right. My baby brother's got a *mean* swing," Big Baby said, grinning at Peanut. "He's the only one of us who can hit our daddy's fast ball. We're all pretty good ballplayers, but Peanut's the best hitter."

"That's right, that's right," Pocket interjected, nodding his head in agreement. "I don't play, but…"—he whipped out a pocket-sized notepad to show Mr. Zip—"I do keep score. See?"

"I *do* see. Very well done, Pocket," said Mr. Zip, patting Pocket on the shoulder. He peered at the notepad, filled with extensive notes and amazingly intricate diagrams.

Pocket beamed with pride, his grin so wide that his normally precise necktie looked almost too tight, and his fitted, button–down shirt appeared as if the buttons might pop off at any moment.

Looking back at Peanut and Big Baby, Mr. Zip said, "I do have a question for you two. How'd you become such good ballplayers?"

"Almost every Saturday, my dad and me and my brothers and sisters go out in the freshly bush-hogged field and play a game of pick-up ball," Peanut replied. "Daddy pitches to us and that's how I became the best hitter." He stopped short, thinking that he might be on the edge of bragging. "Well, 'least that's what they tell me."

Big Baby cuffed Peanut's arm affectionately. "You *know* you are, Peanut. Why do you think Daddy nicknamed you 'Slugger Peanut Johnson' after his ole Louisville Slugger bat?"

Before Peanut could answer, Pocket pulled out his pocket watch. "I hate to interrupt, but we have to go. It's ten o'clock, Big Baby. We need to get home. I have to finish some calculations for the mill."

Big Baby, gentle giant that he was, shrugged. "Okay, Pocket, let's go." Turning to Peanut, he added, "I'll see ya at home, Peanut?"

"Yep, see ya at home."

"See you later, little brother," said Pocket and then turned to Mr. Zip. "It was very nice to make your acquaintance, Mr. Aloysius Zip."

"And yours, Mr. Pocket Johnson," Mr. Zip returned.

With that, the unlikely twosome—Pocket, talking nonstop, and Big Baby, nodding agreeably—pushed open the doors of The Capital Z, leaving Mr. Zip and Peanut in a surprisingly quiet shop.

Peanut grinned, thinking of the unexpected visit. "That's Pocket and Big Baby for you, Mr. Zip. They're almost always together, you know, like peanut butter and jelly. The one sticks with the other."

Still recovering from the whirlwind, Mr. Zip chuckled. "They're quite a duo, that's for sure, but what were we talking about, Peanut? I've lost my place, so to speak."

"Baseball, Mr. Zip, my family and baseball."

"Oh, that's right. We were talking about how good you and your brothers and sisters are at baseball. Why do you think that's so?"

"Well, I guess, because we play every chance we get."

"So, would you say it's because you *practiced* all the time?"

"Yessir, that's what I mean."

"Exactly! So, back to your Uncle Milkweed. Do you think he became so good at shooting…"

At this, Peanut chimed in, "Because he practiced all the time." His face, lighting up in delight, suddenly changed as his eyebrows drew together in a frown. "Yeah, but I still don't get it, Mr. Zip. Why would shooting groundhogs or little chipmunks…"—at this thought, Peanut's voice got a little higher and a little squeakier before trailing off—

"change his life?"

"Just like you're known as 'Slugger Peanut Johnson,' your Uncle Milkweed became known as one of the sharpest marksmen in all of Kentucky and even in Tennessee."

"Wow!" said Peanut, puffing his chest out a little more after hearing of his uncle's fame.

"You already know who Andrew Jackson was because you studied about him in Mrs. Pendergrass's class, right, Peanut?"

"Yep, that's right, Mr. Zip. And I also learned he was the seventh president of the United States."

"Well, before that, did you know that during the War of 1812, Andrew Jackson was a general in the army, stationed in Nashville, Tennessee?"

"No, sir, I don't think I knew that."

"When General Jackson came to Nashville, he had orders to form an army and find some marksmen, some really good sharpshooters. Now, picture this." Mr. Zip put his thumbs together and his pointer fingers straight up, as if to form a picture frame. He stared at something so long, with his eyebrows all scrunched together, that Peanut came up beside him and began to look through the "frame" of Mr. Zip's hands, too.

"On the one hand"—Mr. Zip moved his picture-frame hands to the left—"your uncle's fame as a sharpshooter had begun to spread far and wide." Now he moved the "frame" back to the center. "He had already made the dangerous trip back to Louisiana, purchasing his freedom with his hard-earned 'varmint shooting money' and was living back in Elizabethton, Kentucky, not too far from Nashville. Now, on the other hand"—Mr. Zip said as he moved his "frame" to the right—"there was General Jackson looking for the best sharpshooters all over middle Tennessee, and it was when he heard about Milkweed Johnson," said Mr. Zip, bringing his "frame" once again back to the center, "that he asked for Milkweed to come to Nashville. Now, I don't know if this is how it really happened, but this is how it was told to me."

As Mr. Zip was talking, suddenly standing there in front of Peanut was his great-uncle and General Jackson. Not knowing if what he was seeing was really happening or not, Peanut didn't dare move as he watched…

General Jackson spoke first. "Mr. Johnson, can you hit that knot in yonder pine tree about 150 yards away?"

"I see it, suh," and without another word, Milkweed took aim, his shot crackling through the trees.

General Jackson's scout ran to the tree. When he got there, he yelled back, "Dead center!"

"Mr. Johnson," General Jackson began, "we're going to be traveling all over this country, possibly as far as New Orleans, to fight the British. Would you care to join us?"

Milkweed, seeing his opportunity to get back to the Ormond Plantation to buy his family's freedom, readily agreed. "Yes suh, yes suh, I believe I would."

"That's how the story goes," Mr. Zip said, his silhouette coming back into focus as the image of Peanut's uncle and General Jackson faded from view.

Peanut shook his head. "What just happened?"

Mr. Zip did not seem to notice anything at all unusual and went right on with the story. "From the very beginning, there was trust between the two men."

"Whaat?! But how do you know that, Mr. Zip?" sputtered Peanut, realizing that Mr. Zip was *not* going to answer his *first* question.

"General Jackson found out about your uncle through some people who lived in the area. He learned that Milkweed had already worked many long years—why, close to ten years—just to earn enough money to buy his freedom...and his family's, too."

Peanut was taking it all in, thinking about his uncle, who was now long gone, but brand-new to him.

"Your Uncle Milkweed also knew he could trust General Jackson," Mr. Zip continued.

"Really?" Peanut asked, raising his eyebrows.

"Yes, indeed. During the War of 1812, Jackson was commissioned as General over the Tennessee Militia and was ordered to go to New Orleans to defend America against the British. But he had only gone partway when the War Department ordered him back. Can you believe it? But wait..."—Mr. Zip pointed his long, bony index finger into the air—"there's more. Not only did they order him back, they also told him to disband his army and send them home without pay."

"That's not right, Mr. Zip!"

"You'd better believe it was not right, Peanut. General Jackson was outraged! He felt his men were being treated unfairly, but on top of that, if he disbanded them…if he left them where they were…their lives would be in danger."

"Uh…but how would they be in danger, Mr. Zip? It seems to me they would be safer at home than fighting in a war."

"Yes, that would be true except his men had to go back through the dangerous Indian Territory they had just crossed. To disband would mean that each man was on his own—not a good thing in Indian Territory. So, do you know what Jackson did?"

Peanut shrugged. "What could he do? He had his orders."

"He did the only thing he could do. He marched them back," Mr. Zip folded his arms and took a defiant stance, "paying out of his own pocket, to bring his men home."[2]

"Wow!" Peanut was pretty awestruck.

"Do you know what that did for his men? His men knew that, no matter what, General Jackson was there for them, would stay with them, endure anything and everything alongside them. Because of that, they loved and deeply respected him. Why, they thought he was as tough as an old hickory tree…so they nicknamed him 'Old Hickory.'"

Peanut was amazed. "I don't think I know anyone who would do that…even if they could."

"Yep, Old Hickory was loyal to his men and loyal to his country. So, your Uncle Milkweed became a sharpshooter for General Jackson, following him into many more battles, the last one, ironically, the battle of New Orleans. General Jackson defeated the British on December 1, 1814, bringing the War of 1812 to an end. Everyone started home…that is, almost everyone."

"Why not everyone?"

"Remember, your Uncle Milkweed's family was at the Ormond Plantation, not too far from New Orleans. Well, at the end of the war—at least, this is the story that has been passed down through generations—just at sunset one cold, December evening, your Uncle Milkweed came to see the General. He approached Jackson's assistant, the sergeant on duty."

Once again, what Mr. Zip was saying began to take shape in front of Peanut. This is what he saw and heard:

"Please, suh, I needs to speak with de Major Gen'ral," Milkweed asked.

"Wait here just a minute," the sergeant replied respectfully.

In just a few seconds, General Jackson appeared. Walking over and taking a smoldering stick from the campfire to light his pipe, he motioned to Milkweed. "Walk with me, Mr. Johnson."

The army was camped near a river. Mr. Zip, who was still standing beside Peanut, whispered, "They're on the banks of the Mississippi River." Peanut nodded in silent amazement as more and more of the scene unfolded before his very eyes.

The sky was the dark slate blue of twilight, and just at the horizon, remnants of pink were all that were left of the day. A sliver of the moon and a few young evening stars were just beginning to come out in the night sky. Uncle Milkweed and Old Hickory walked for a few moments without saying a word.

Jackson spoke first. "What's on your mind, Mr. Johnson?"

"Well, Major Gen'ral, suh, I left my fambly here in Looisiana when I made it to freedom in Kaintuck."

"Yes sir, Mr. Johnson, I remember."

"Well, suh, I never meant to leave my fambly fer good, Major Gen'ral, suh. I allus planned on a-comin' back one day. I did all sohts o' odd jobs earnin' money any ways I could. Why, dat's how I came to be sich a good shootuh, iffen yo' don' mind me sayin' so."

Milkweed fidgeted with his hat. "I was workin' on de fust fahm, Mr. McClendon's place, shootin' varmints. I got real good at it, too, and mo' and mo' farmers come to hire me to clear de fields. Yes, suh, dey did and dey paid me. Dey paid me real good and I saved all de money so I could come back one day and buy my fambly's freedom. Yes, suh, I did, 'cause I had already come back and paid my massuh for my freedom, suh, Um hm. But now, I needs yo' hep, Major Gen'ral, suh. I was ahopin' dat mebbe you could hep me figgur a way to go back and talk with da massuh about buyin' my fambly's freedom."

Old Hickory paused for a few seconds, thinking about what Milkweed had just told him. "Well, Mr. Johnson, I don't think I rightly understand why you need my help. You bought your own freedom, right?"

"Yes, suh, yes, suh, I did, suh. But de problem is dat de Trépagnier Plantation now has a new massuh who don' know me and who don' knows I done bought my freedom. I need yo' hep to tell my story."

"I understand. You do have your freedom papers though, correct?"

"Yes, suh, yes, suh, I do...." Milkweed's voice trailed off.

The two men walked quietly along for a few more minutes. They stopped under a sycamore tree, Jackson puffing on his pipe.

"Mr. Johnson, you have served with me for over a year now. You are an honorable man, a man I trust. You remind me of my blacksmith, Ned. It would be my honor to go with you and help you. We'll get your family back for you." *

With those words, the images of Milkweed and General Jackson began to fade, and once again, Peanut was standing in The This and That Shop with Mr. Zip.

"So, that's what happened, Peanut. Your Uncle Milkweed rode with Jackson to the Ormond Plantation. With the General by his side, your uncle was able to buy his whole family's freedom and return to Kentucky. So, let that be a lesson to you!"

"Huh? What just happened? Mr. Zip...my great-great-great-great uncle...and he was talking! And he was talking different. Why?"

"Whoa, slow down Peanut. The reason he sounded different was because he was truly just learning to speak the English language. Quite an accomplishment, don't you think?"

"I hadn't thought of that. Wow, that's really good. I can speak *only* English."

"Me, too, Peanut. But let's get back to what we were talking about. Oh, yes! What did I tell you that totally changed your uncle's life?"

"He...shot varmints, clearing off farmers' fields...."

"That's right. That's part of it, Peanut. Go on."

Peanut thought for a moment, then added, "My uncle got really good at shooting the critters...and because he was so good..."—in his growing excitement, he spoke faster and faster, his words tumbling over each other—"he became a sharpshooter for General Jackson, who ended up bringing him back to New Orleans and then took him to the plantation to buy his family's freedom! I see now, Mr. Zip! Shootin' varmints really did change his life!" Then more softly, he added, "My uncle really was a good man, wasn't he, Mr. Zip?"

"Not only good, Peanut, but also faithful and brave. He was faithful because he always did what he said he was going to do. He was brave, not only because he fought in the war, but because he dared to go back to Louisiana even though he could have been recaptured and forced to live out the rest of his life as a slave."

Peanut grew very still. The cuckoo clock's ticking was the only sound that could be heard inside The Capital Z. Mr. Zip thought he could detect in Peanut's sincerely polite and deeply brown eyes, pride for his uncle, but also, maybe…a little sadness. Before Mr. Zip could say anything, Peanut closed his eyes and shook his head once more, as if to shake off something he didn't want to remember.

Taking a deep breath as he reopened his eyes, Peanut said, "I think I'll look around a little more, if you don't mind, Mr. Zip."

"Why, of course not, Peanut. Let me know if you have questions about anything else." Mr. Zip started back toward his desk, but watching Peanut out of the corner of his eye, thought he noticed something a little different about him.

Maybe it was because Peanut Johnson had just discovered that he had a very brave great-great-great-great-uncle or maybe it was because his uncle was highly respected by a war hero, who later became president! But whatever the reason, Peanut seemed to walk a little taller and hold his head a little higher than when he had first entered The This and That Shop. Mr. Zip smiled.

* The speech patterns of Milkweed were found in *Born in Slavery: Slave Narratives from the Federal Writers' Project, 1936-1938,* This narrative contains more than 2,300 first-person accounts of slavery and 500 black-and-white photographs of former slaves collected as part of the Federal Writers' Project of the Works Progress Administration.

Did You Know

…that runaway slaves did go back and buy their freedom, but would often travel with white people to keep from being recaptured by slave-catchers?

Chapter 3

General Washington Runs Away

As Peanut Johnson strolled around the shop, thinking about his Uncle Milkweed, his fingers absently gliding over items that at any other time would surely have caught his attention, he stopped when he saw a beautiful sword hanging on the wall. Walking over to it and seeing the nameplate, his eyes bounced open in amazement.

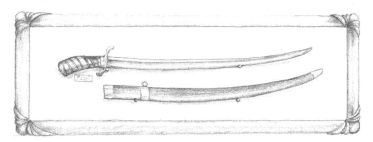

First, forming the words with his mouth, he gasped, "George...Washington?" He raised his voice so Mr. Zip could hear. "Mr. Zip, is this *really* George Washington's sword?" (Because, remember, the Kentucky rifle really *did* belong to Peanut's Great-Great-Great-Great-Uncle Milkweed!)

Mr. Zip had already sat down at his desk, but in a jiffy was at Peanut's side, carefully removing the sword from the wall.

"No, Peanut, this is what I call 'a reminder' of George Washington's sword. The real one hangs in the Smithsonian Institute in Washington, DC. This sword reminds me of who George Washington was as a person and what he believed in."

"Huh?" Once again, Peanut Johnson took on that quizzical look that was beginning to be at home on his face the longer he stayed in The Capital Z.

"In fact, most of the things in this shop are reminders," Mr. Zip went on without missing a beat. Walking around the shop, he began to point out various artifacts giving a short history of each one. He touched the ship that was displayed on a pedestal with a plaque that read: "World War II." Then the diver's mask: "The first deep sea diving expedition." From the way he was talking, it seemed to Peanut that Mr. Zip had a firsthand knowledge, almost as if he had actually been there! *No way.* Dismissing the thought as quickly as it had entered his head, Peanut caught up to what Mr. Zip was saying.

"I call the things in this shop 'reminders' because they help us to remember our history. They remind us of who we are, what we believe, and where we came from. For instance, this sword tells us that Washington was a military man, but it also opens the door for us to see a little more of who he was as a person—that is, if we're curious enough to find out." Allowing his words to hang in the air, Mr. Zip peeked over at Peanut to see if his comment had sparked any curiosity.

Peanut mumbled a distracted "Uh-huh" and continued to focus on the sword.

"Some of these memorabilia also remind us of good times, but others, of times that weren't so good. As a matter of fact, some of those times were incredibly hard. You know, Peanut, it's when times are not so good, when things seem incredibly hard, that we become stronger."

This *really* caught Peanut's attention. "Oh," he said, looking up, the smile on his face fading and sadness creeping back into his brown eyes.

Mr. Zip placed his hand carefully, almost tenderly, on Peanut's shoulder. "What is it, son?"

Peanut sighed deeply and his shoulder sagged a little lower. It was not the weight of Mr. Zip's hand that made Peanut's shoulder sag, but the weight of what had happened the day before yesterday.

"Do you want to talk about it, Peanut?"

It took a minute for Peanut to gather up the courage to face this kind, older gentleman. "Mr. Zip, have you ever done anything that you wish you could go back and undo?" Peanut stared at the floor, because he did not want Mr. Zip to see that tears were forming in his eyes.

"Oh, we all have, Peanut." Mr. Zip's voice trailed off, leaving a peace-filled quiet that invited Peanut to continue.

"Even George Washington?" Peanut asked, looking at the sword and blinking back the tears. "Like when he cut down the cherry tree?"

Mr. Zip chuckled softly and his eyes twinkled. "Yes, Peanut, even George Washington. But I'm not thinking about the cherry tree story right now."

"Well, then what? He couldn't have done anything else wrong, right, Mr. Zip? He was the best! Isn't that what made him president...because he was the best? He was the best general. He was the best because he won the war!" The pace of Peanut's words quickened with each thought.

"Slow down, Peanut. You're right. He was the best, but George Washington would be the first to tell you that he didn't do everything right."

"But George Washington's the Father of our Country! He had to have done everything right," Peanut protested.

"Calm down, Peanut. Yes, he *is* the Father of our Country, but not because he was perfect or because he was a great general or even a great president. I believe it was because of *who* George Washington was at the core of his heart that made him great."

"I don't understand what you mean, Mr. Zip."

"Have you ever known someone who would not admit when they had done something wrong, or who wouldn't take responsibility for a mistake they knew they had made?"

"Yessir..." Peanut offered half-heartedly, not knowing where Mr. Zip was heading.

"Well, me too, but George Washington was not that kind of man. In fact, he would be the first to tell you that he made mistakes, even big ones." Mr. Zip rearranged his long frame and made himself comfortable at his desk. "Let me tell you about a famous battle between George Washington and General Howe during the American War of Independence, the Revolutionary War. At that time, Washington was a general. In March of 1776, while Washington was fighting the Redcoats in New York, he found he had put himself in an *untenable* position."[3] Seeing the questioning look in Peanut's eyes, he paused, suspecting that the word *untenable* had gone right over his young friend's head. "Oh, I'm sorry, Peanut...I mean, that George Washington had put himself and his troops in a place he couldn't defend."

"Oh, okay," said Peanut. "So...what happened next?"

"Well, shucks...let me SHOW you!" Mr. Zip jumped up and, in a tangle of arms and legs, scrambled to the shelf above them. Barely able to peek over that shelf, Mr. Zip stretched as far as he could, becoming more wiry than Peanut thought was humanly possible. He grabbed at something long that appeared to be rolled up and quite dusty. Pulling down the unknown object, clouds of dust flew EVERYWHERE and Peanut began to sneeze–violently!

"Achoo! Achoo! Achoo!" His sneezes were so loud that Mr. Zip thought Peanut would positively turn himself inside out.

"My goodness! Bless you!" said Mr. Zip, jumping down and unrolling a parchment on which was drawn a map of New England. "Look, Peanut." Pointing his long, bony finger at Brooklyn, he went on. "George Washington's army was *here* and General William Howe's forces were on the land and water, which were here and here." Mr. Zip moved his finger to the spot where General Howe's men were situated.

Peanut could see that Brooklyn was just east of the Hudson River. He could also see how General Howe could attack General Washington from the river on one side and from land on the other. "This was the 'un-ten-a-ble' position, right, Mr. Zip?" Peanut smiled as he slowly mastered the new word.

"Yes, Peanut, but do you know what General Washington did?"

"Well, probably...because he was smart and a good army man, I bet..." began Peanut, thinking out loud, and then adding as the idea struck him, "I know! I bet he sent spies to come up with a plan for a secret, surprise attack! Right, Mr. Zip?"

"Nope, not exactly, Peanut. Guess again."

"Well, then...maybe he hid?" Peanut replied, a little more hesitantly this time.

"Nope! That's a little better guess, but you'll never believe what he did do. He *ran!*" Mr. Zip winked, knowing that his answer was not what Peanut expected.

"What?!"

"Yes, Peanut, he *ran!* He took his army and retreated from Manhattan into Westchester County, moving through New Jersey all the way into Pennsylvania," said Mr. Zip, tracing on the map General Washington's path.

"Whoa!" Peanut stepped back from the map for a better look at how far George Washington had to go.

"Peanut, General Washington actually saved his army by turning back. Putting his troops in the untenable position in the first place was a bad decision, but having them march all that way, only to have them retreat with great haste—Peanut, you could even say they had to flee—meant that his already weary men suffered even more."

"Oh, Mr. Zip, that's terrible."

"Did you know, on top of this, that his men were ill-clothed, and many of them didn't even have boots to wear? And that most of the time, Peanut, they barely had even enough food to survive?"

"No sir, I did not know that. That's awful."

"It was awful, but in the end, Peanut, it was what George Washington *did* that mattered." Mr. Zip paused.

"Do you think, Peanut, that General Washington felt badly about what had happened to his men and that he was deeply sorry for his poor judgment? Do you think he might have questioned whether he was the right man for the job or whether he was even good enough to lead? Do you think that because people were counting on him, he felt he had let them down?"

As Mr. Zip spoke, it was as if his words draped themselves around Peanut's already sagging shoulders, reminding him of what had happened that he wished had never happened.

After a moment, Peanut spoke so softly that Mr. Zip could barely hear him. "I think...I *know*...how he felt."

...that George Washington's troops escaped across the East River in August of 1776 through a very thick and unnatural fog? That thick, unnatural fog is actually documented in the memoirs of Major Benjamin Tallmadge, who was with the last troops to leave the island that day![4]

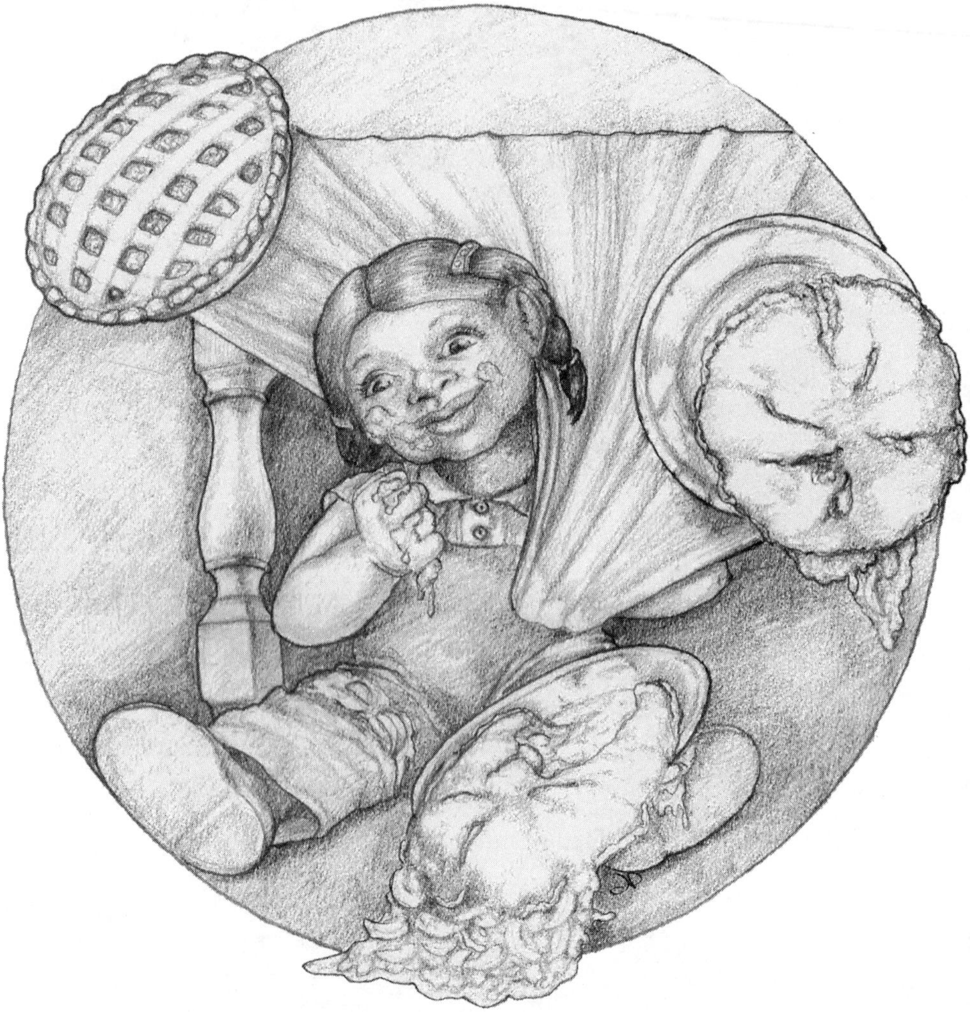

Chapter 4

Lovie Dovie and the Peach Pie Plate

M r. Zip sat down on his stool so that he and Peanut were face to face. "What are you holding onto, Peanut?" he asked kindly. "What's troubling you?"

Peanut sighed deeply. "Day before yesterday, everything was just right. My whole family—Mama, Daddy, Secret, Big Baby, Pocket, Royal, and Whisper—all of us were so excited about getting ready for the Fourth of July Parade in town. Mama was baking all sorts of pies—apple pies, cherry pies, and her award-winning peach pies." Peanut smiled at the thought.

"I've tasted her peach pies," said Mr. Zip. "They're mighty good!"

Peanut nodded. "My daddy has the responsibility of putting up the town bleachers every year for the Fourth of July. You see, Mr. Zip, my daddy's the supervisor at the sawmill."

"Yes, I know. And setting up those bleachers is a very important responsibility."

"On the day before the Fourth, Daddy loads our whole family into the Model T truck to go help."

"Why, excuse me for interrupting, Peanut...but a Model T truck?"

"Yessir, Mr. Zip, a really *old* Model T truck," said Peanut, nodding in agreement.

"Why, Peanut, that truck must be *really* old." For once, Mr. Zip appeared to be gen-u-ine-ly, pos-i-tive-ly taken aback.

"Our Model T has been in the family a long, long time—before I was even born!"

"That is amazing, truly amazing, Peanut."

"What's amazing, Mr. Zip?"

"That the old truck is still running."

Brushing aside Mr. Zip's comment, Peanut continued, "Yes, well, everyone was in the Model T—that is, everyone but Lovie Dovie and me."

"Lovie Dovie?"

"Lovie Dovie's the baby of the family. You know that, Mr. Zip."

"Oh, yes, that's right. I remember. Go on."

"Well, everyone had piled into the truck to go into town, and Mama and Daddy left me in charge of watching Lovie Dovie. Now, it's only a ten-minute trip into town—or that's all it *should* be—but my daddy, being so proud of his Model T truck and all, kept stopping along the way to pick up folks walking into town, 'specially because it was such a hot day."

"It was certainly very hot that day, so that was very nice of your daddy. Shows he's a good man."

"Yessir, but my mama gets flustered when my daddy

does that because the Model T truck gets so packed with people—like a can of sardines—that sometimes a tire goes flat. And you know, Mr. Zip, that's just what happened. Sure 'nough, one of the tires went flat—kersplat!" Peanut clapped his hands for emphasis.

"Everyone had to pile out of the truck while someone ran to get the tire fixed. Then the men had to change the tire. It took *hours* to fix that tire and put it back on the truck, and, on top of it all, to go put up those risers. And there I was all that time—stuck at home watching Lovie Dovie," Peanut said with exasperation and began fidgeting with the corner of the map, still lying open on the table.

"Go on, go on. What happened after that?"

"Well," he began hesitantly, "Lovie Dovie is only three years old, so she loves to play with little puzzles. Day before yesterday, she was sitting on the floor, playing with one of her wooden puzzles. I could tell she was real happy too, because she was humming and singing. When she was a little baby, while Mama would feed her in her high chair, Lovie would kinda hum and yum every time she took a bite. Yessir, she would hum and yum over smashed-up green peas! Now *that's* something I just don't understand. Yuck!" Peanut shook his head in disgust.

"You know what else, Mr. Zip?" Without waiting for an answer, Peanut hurried on. "Lovie Dovie puts the puzzles together, pats the pieces down with her little hands, and then turns all the puzzles upside down again. Then she throws her arms over her head and starts laughin'. I really don't get that." Peanut rolled his sincerely polite, big brown eyes.

"It was *so* boring, Mr. Zip, just watching Lovie Dovie all afternoon. And it was *so* hot, too. Lovie wasn't paying any attention to me, so I decided to go out back, hoping to catch a fresh breeze. But first, I made sure I locked the front screen with the hook because I surely didn't want Lovie Dovie going out the front door. No sir, 'specially with me in the backyard," Peanut said. "When I went out, I listened to make sure the screen door slapped shut behind me. When I heard it slap shut, I just knew Lovie Dovie would be okay."

Peanut's eyes took on a faraway look as if he had gone out the back door again and said, with a wistful sigh, "When I went outside, there she was—the prettiest girl you ever did see, Mr. Zip—Mary Bell Juniper.

"Oh, she's sweet, Mr. Zip—*real* sweet. She's got the prettiest eyes that sparkle whenever she talks and the prettiest caramel-colored skin. Oh, Mr. Zip, she's honey, but the bees don't know it." Gazing off dreamily into the distance, thinking about Mary Bell Juniper, Peanut suddenly threw his head back and, with all of his heart and at the top of his voice, he exclaimed, "She's honeey, but the bees don't know it!"

"What did you say?" asked Mr. Zip, chuckling out loud, his eyes twinkling because it was clear that Peanut Johnson was quite taken with Mary Bell Juniper, the prettiest girl in the whole wide world! "Does she know you think she's honey but the bees don't know it?"

"Oh, yessir, Mr. Zip! Sometimes, I walk across the top of her picket fence and yell it to her window." Just thinking about Mary Bell Juniper made Peanut's heart leap like a frog while his knees turned to jelly. "Oh, Mr. Zip, she's the best! Yessir, she's honeeey, but the bees don't know it... umm, umm, umm."

But as Peanut stood there, the broad smile that extended from corner to corner of his expressive mouth began to disappear. "But guess that doesn't matter too much...not after what happened. Oh, me!" Peanut groaned, putting his forehead in his hands. "Why, oh, why didn't I do what I was supposed to do?"

"Why, Peanut, it can't be all that bad."

"Remember how Lovie Dovie was inside playing with her puzzles while Mary Bell Juniper and I were outside under the oak tree, just talking and visiting? Seemed like no time at all had passed until I realized I didn't hear anything from inside the house, 'specially not Lovie Dovie humming or laughing...."

Peanut became quiet for a moment.

"Mr. Zip, when I didn't hear anything, I jumped up

from leaning on the picket fence and ran toward the house. 'Mary Bell, Mary Bell!' I yelled back to her. 'I've got to go see about my little sister!'

"I ran to the back screen door and yanked it open, all the while calling, 'Lovie Dovie, Lovie Dovie!' After being outside in that bright sunlight, though, I couldn't see a thing. But I sure could hear moanin' and whimperin'"—he paused, looking at Mr. Zip with a woebegone expression on his face—"you know, kinda like a little kitty crying." Peanut's eyes filled with fear.

"I kept calling, 'Lovie Dovie, Lovie Dovie, where are you?' I ran to the kitchen, but all I found were broken pie plates and pie all over the floor. I searched the family room next, but she wasn't there, either. I finally found her curled up in one of the bedroom closets. Piecrusts, peaches, and cherries were all in her hair and around her mouth. I had just found her when Mama and Daddy burst into the room. I hadn't even heard them come home.

"'What happened?' Mama cried.

"Daddy ran past me and, with Mama following close behind, scooped Lovie Dovie from my arms and hollered, 'Crank up the model T, Royal! We have to take Lovie Dovie into town to see Doc Earl!'

"Mama was almost out the door when she stopped, turned around, and walked back over. Kneeling down so she was looking into my eyes, she took me by both shoulders and said, 'Peanut, you need to clean up this mess and wait here quietly. We'll be home in a little while.'

"Mr. Zip, Mama's eyes were really sad." Peanut studied Mr. Zip's expression, hoping for a tiny bit of comfort.

"Oh, I know Lovie Dovie's okay because I didn't hear any bad news yesterday," Mr. Zip said gently, "and believe me, I do know the news of this town. But please, go on with your story."

"Well, I cleaned up the broken pie plates and all the crumbs and stains best I could. But even though my brothers and sisters came in and stayed with me, there was not much talking. Big Baby kinda walked over to me and punched my shoulder as if to tell me everything would be okay. Whisper gave me a hug. But everyone else was real quiet. We just waited and waited and waited.

"By the time Mama and Daddy walked through the door, it was real late. Lovie Dovie was asleep in Daddy's arms. She did have a few small cuts from the glass pie plates and a huge stomach ache from eating all those pies, but she was okay." Peanut shook his head sadly.

"All of us were so worn out, we just went to bed. But I didn't sleep much that night. I tossed and turned and had fitful dreams, mostly about looking for Lovie Dovie in the dark. When morning came, everyone got up, but no one said anything. There was no laughing and joking around like there usually is on the Fourth of July. That's when Daddy called me to him."

Now, Peanut's daddy, Early Johnson, had a really deep bass voice—not a rough deep bass, but a velvety deep bass—so musical and comforting, you could be lulled to sleep. Yet, at other times, it was so commanding, you didn't dare move...not even an inch! When Early called Peanut to talk with him, it was one of *those* times.

Peanut began to tell Mr. Zip, word for word, what his daddy had said to him. As he talked, it was as if Peanut were standing in front of his daddy...the day before yesterday...

"Peanut, son, you know your Mama and I were real disappointed with what happened yesterday."

"Yessir." *Peanut nodded in agreement, his head bent low because he felt so bad about everything.*

"You know that even though Lovie Dovie is all right, and we are grateful to the Good Lord for that, she will have to be carried around the whole day and won't enjoy much of the Fourth of July festivities."

*Daddy cleared his throat, and Peanut held his breath, bracing himself for what his dad would say next. This was serious—*real *serious.* *"And you know, son,"* *Daddy went on,* *"that the bonus I get every year for putting up those bleachers will have to be used to pay all the doctor's bills from last night."*

"Yessir," *Peanut said, still staring at his feet.*

"But did you know that all the money your Mama usually makes with her award-winning pies won't be coming in this year, and she won't get the joy of watching people's faces light up when they taste her pies?"

"No, sir. Guess I didn't think of that." *Peanut's voice dropped to a whisper.*

"But sadly, son, the biggest hurt in all this, is the hurt you did to yourself."

Peanut looked up questioningly.

"You may have let your Mama and me down yesterday...for that matter, your whole family, especially Lovie Dovie. But mostly, you let yourself down. We gave you a job, a responsibility. We were counting on you to take care of Lovie Dovie since she's too little to take care of herself. Now, I know it was hot and I know you were disappointed at being left here with your baby sister, but each one of us had a job to do. We are a family and we work together. And now, well, look at what has happened."

Peanut's dad paused for a moment to give Peanut a chance to think about what he had just said. "Peanut, there are always consequences for our actions, as you have seen, but there has to be a direct consequence for you."

Oh, no. *Peanut's heart sank.* Here it comes!

"I understand from Mrs. Juniper that you spent a great deal of time at the picket fence talking to a special little lady yesterday afternoon."

Peanut gulped.

Mr. Johnson continued. "That picket fence surely is in need of some paint, and it seems to me that since you enjoyed spending so much time there yesterday, you wouldn't mind spending your Fourth of July, painting the entire fence."

Peanut's eyes got big. "You mean the whole fence, even the Junipers' side?"

"I mean the whole *fence," said Daddy, clearly and firmly. "That way you will have plenty of time to think about yesterday."*

"And so," said Peanut, returning from his mental replay of what had happened on the Fourth of July, "that was my yesterday. Everyone went off to the parade and picnic afterward, and I spent the day painting that fence. Do you know what was even worse, Mr. Zip? While I was outside painting, Clayton Clayborn came to Mary Bell Juniper's house to take her to the parade. Oh my, she looked so pretty, too, but I could barely look at her. I was so ashamed."

Mr. Zip stood there for a moment, seemingly gazing into thin air. He walked over to a shelf across the room. What Mr. Zip did next seemed rather odd, but as if he were expecting someone, he picked up *three* tricorne hats. He had just opened his mouth to say something when the bells above those old, arched oak doors began to jingle, announcing that someone had just entered The Capital Z.

Peanut took a closer look. Someone *had* come in, all right. Not just anyone, mind you...but Bear Berpowsky!

…that the Model T, built by the Ford Motor Company from 1908-1927, had a nickname? It was called the "Tin Lizzie" or "flivver."[5]

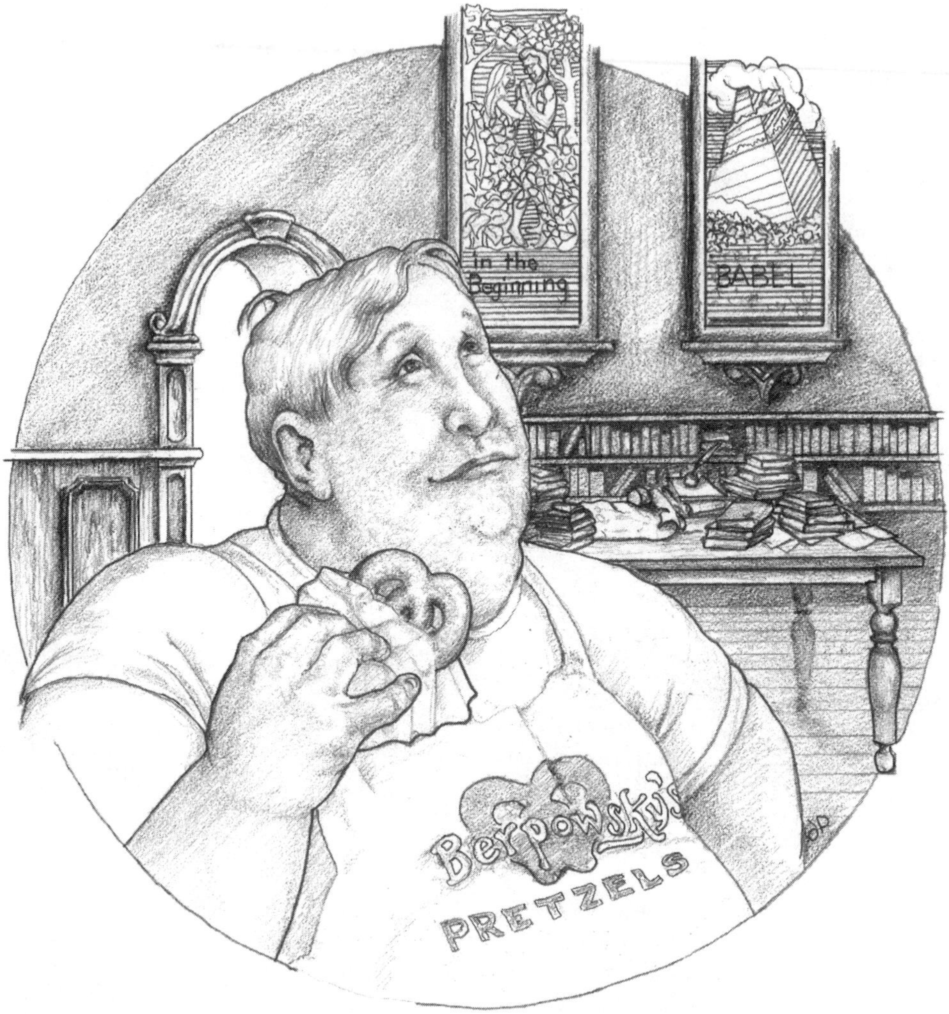
In the Beginning
BABEL
Berpowsky's
PRETZELS

Chapter 5

Bear Berpowsky
and the Stained-Glass Stories

B ear Berpowsky literally fit into his name. Not really a terribly big fellow, almost everything about him resembled a bear, from his rather large head sitting atop broad shoulders to his stocky arms attached, seemingly without wrists, to his hands. But mostly, it was the way he walked, much like a bear lumbering along as if he didn't have a care in the world. Bear owned the pretzel stand on the street corner right outside The Capital Z, and besides being a good friend of Mr. Zip, he always seemed to show up "just in time."

So when Mr. Zip looked up to see Bear coming through the door, he gave him a wide grin and said, "You're just in time!" With that and a sweeping gesture, he signaled to Peanut and Bear, shouting, "Follow me!" Mr. Zip was moving so quickly, it seemed as if his words trailed behind in somewhat of an echo as Peanut and Bear chased after him to catch up.

Mr. Zip, who appeared to be all arms and legs, zipped from the front of the shop, through the hallway, and burst into the back room of The Capital Z, coming to a sudden halt. Bear, who was excited about their next adventure, and Peanut, close behind, almost fell over each other as they found themselves in the most magnificent room Peanut had ever seen.

Peanut's mouth dropped open in awe as he murmured, "Wow." Beyond that, he did not, could not, say another word. Bear stood beside Peanut, taking it all in as he had so many times before.

The room was about three stories high. It was not filled with the fine antiques you might expect, but with books—books that lined the walls from floor to ceiling. Even though the room was grand, it was warm and welcoming and smelled of comfortable leather sofas, cherry pipe tobacco, and fires from winter days. But most of all, this room seemed to hold memories of long ago and tales yet to be told.

On a stand on the left side of the room was a worn Spanish saddle. Mr. Zip did not have a horse, so this was rather odd since the saddle appeared to have been recently used. Books, casually left open, were spread out on an old, knotty pine table, which stood in the middle of the room. In the far corner was a stone fireplace with an opening so expansive that if they wanted to, both Bear and Peanut could have stood inside it, fully upright. Nearby were two plush sofas. They looked so comfortable that Peanut thought if you sat in one, you might feel like you were sinking into a cloud.

Colorful lights dancing around the room caught Peanut's eye. Tilting his head back, he counted seven stained-glass windows. "These are the most beautiful windows I've ever seen, Mr. Zip."

Joining Bear and Peanut, Mr. Zip spoke almost reverently, "Each stained-glass window tells a story, so I call them 'stained-glass stories.'"

Bear smiled. "You know, Mr. Zip," he drawled, "I think that a better name for them is 'stained-glass reminders.'"

Knowing that Bear was a wise man, Mr. Zip agreed. "You're right, Bear. They *are* reminders." He pointed to the first window. "This one is of Adam and Eve, the very first man and woman created by God, in the Garden of Eden. The Bible tells us that the Garden was without sin. In other words, it was perfect in every way—perfect climate, perfect temperature, perfect people. There were bugs and animals, to be sure, but because sin was not a part of the Garden of Eden, there was only goodness there."

"What do you mean, Mr. Zip?" asked Peanut.

"Well, for example, there were wasps, but because there was no sin, they didn't try to sting you. Lions were as friendly as puppies. Why, even cats and dogs got along quite famously."

The whole time Mr. Zip was talking, Peanut was studying this "stained-glass story." He noticed that even though Adam and Eve were not wearing any clothes, it didn't seem to matter. They were just gazing into each other's eyes, holding hands. In fact, Peanut thought it was the nicest picture he had ever seen of the first couple on earth.

"They look so innocent…and so *happy,*" said Peanut, a little surprised.

"Why, yes, Peanut. Because sin had not entered the world, Adam and Eve were not ashamed or afraid. They didn't even know what fear was. Imagine…wouldn't that be something…to not be afraid? They only knew that God loved them."

Walking over to the next window, with Bear and Peanut following, Mr. Zip continued, "This one shows the story of Noah and the great Flood. Do you know about the Flood, Peanut?"

"Why, yessir, Noah built a HUGE ark"—Peanut stretched his arms as wide apart as possible—"and he brought in every animal, two by two."

Mr. Zip smiled. "Well, you're right, but why did he do that?"

Peanut frowned, thinking Mr. Zip should certainly know the answer to *that* question. "God told him to because God was going to send the Flood, the BIG FLOOD, that's why."

"Well, yes, Peanut," Mr. Zip said, chuckling because he could see Peanut's frustration. "But what I mean is, why did God send the Flood?"

"My daddy told me it was because evil—the worst meanness ever—was taking over the earth and God had to get rid of it."

"That's right. The same meanness that came along when sin entered the world had grown and grown, and God decided to begin again. Pretty interesting when you think about it, huh, boys?" Mr. Zip paused as Bear shuffled his feet and Peanut looked down in thought. "Do you think it was because God loved us so much that He wanted to get rid of as much evil as possible?"

"I hadn't thought of it that way before, Mr. Zip," said Peanut, "but what about all the people that weren't on the ark? Didn't God love them, too?"

"Yes, most definitely. God instructed Noah to tell everyone that a big flood was coming and, if they wanted to survive, they should get on the ark with Noah and his family. God always offers a way of escape, you see."

Peanut was quiet for a few moments, letting what Mr. Zip had just said sink in for a bit. Then, eager to get on with the stories, he ran over to the next stained-glass window, with Bear and Mr. Zip in tow. Looking up, he said, "I don't know what this story is all about, Mr. Zip. It just looks like a tall tower surrounded by a bunch of people to me."

"Why, that's the Tower of Babel," said Bear.

"The Tower of Babel?" Peanut's forehead creased in a frown.

Mr. Zip nodded. "Many years after  the great Flood, some of Noah's descendants settled in the land of Shinar that later became known as Babylon. Those early Babylonians began to build a great city and a magnificent tower that reached to the sky. You know, I don't think people today have any idea how tall that tower was or how smart those Babylonians were...."

As Mr. Zip talked, Peanut suddenly found himself standing in a great crowd of people, looking up at an incredibly tall tower, Bear and Mr. Zip next to him.

Frightened, Peanut grabbed Mr. Zip's arm, and sputtered, "Mr. Zip, Mr. Zip, what's happening?"

Mr. Zip continued talking as if nothing were out of the ordinary. "Don't worry, Peanut. You're here with me, and we're just watching a piece of history unfold, much like we would watch a movie."

Peanut clutched Mr. Zip's arm even more tightly. As they stood there, the people all around them were celebrating, pointing up at the awesome structure. "Look what we built!" Peanut heard someone say. Another replied, "Nothing like this has ever been done before!" Then another, "Now we are invincible! Even a great flood could never reach this high! We will be greater than God!"

The boasting grew louder and louder, so loud that it became a roar. Peanut could hardly stand it. He put his fingers in his ears, trying to quiet the noise. But just as he did, everything stopped. The laughter stopped. The talking stopped. Everyone seemed to be shocked into a stunned and helpless silence. It was as if no one even dared move...or breathe.

All at once, everyone began talking again, but not with the happy laughter or boasting as before, but with yelling, and then terrified screaming. Confusion and panic began to rip through the crowd.

The person next to Peanut was shouting what Peanut thought sounded like French, another screaming Chinese—each trying desperately to get the other to understand. Fighting broke out and people, as if fleeing for their lives, began to run in all directions.

Some ran right past Peanut and, to his astonishment, disappeared in the distance! At the same time, the tumult began to die, like dust settling to the ground after a storm.

Peanut was suddenly aware that Mr. Zip was calmly talking as if nothing were the slightest bit unusual. When he looked around, he saw that they were once again mysteriously back inside The This and That Shop.

"It must have been a terribly heartbreaking and frightening time," Mr. Zip continued.

Peanut was still holding Mr. Zip's arm as if his life depended on it. "Mr. Zip, what was that? What just happened?"

"It's like I said, son—we just witnessed another bit of history, that's all." Mr. Zip paused for a second. "Now, where was I? People who had fled each other in terror—think about it, Peanut, maybe even families and close friends—now felt very isolated and very alone. How do you think you would have felt if you had been there?"

Peanut, his eyes like saucers, was still in shock. "I'd be afraid, Mr. Zip, because, well…see…you don't know what's going to happen next! Yessir, Mr. Zip, I'd be REAL afraid!"

"People *were* afraid, Peanut, and it was that fear that caused them to become suspicious of everything and everyone. Over time, fear began to give way to superstition, and superstition began to take the place of God. In fact, most people forgot about God completely, and the little that others remembered was swallowed up in old sayings and vague whisperings. But do you know what, Peanut?" Mr. Zip asked, his eyes twinkling more brightly than ever. "God had a plan. He always has a plan."

Bear broke into the conversation with a heartfelt "AMEN!"

Peanut stood there for a moment, dumbfounded, looking back and forth between the two men. He could not believe that Mr. Zip and Bear were not as affected by what had just happened as he was! He had just lifted his pointer finger and was about to say something when the stained-glass window at the end of the room caught his eye, causing him to forget what he had just seen. Racing toward it, Peanut said, "Whoa, Mr. Zip! Look at *that!*"

This window was larger than the others and Peanut thought of all the ones he had seen, it was the most beautiful. In the very center was a stained-glass cross.

Coming up behind Peanut, Mr. Zip said quietly, "This is my favorite. It is lovely, isn't it?"

From Mr. Zip's hushed tone, Peanut could tell that this window meant a lot to him. Almost in a whisper, Peanut asked, "Why do you like it so much?"

"Well, I'm a Christian, Peanut, and this cross is a reminder of how much God loves me…."

"Me, too," Bear added, his deep, rumbly voice now very soft.

Mr. Zip, Bear, and Peanut stood there looking at the

cross, each one alone with his thoughts. Peanut was thinking about what Mr. Zip had just said and was wondering what he meant when...

Surprisingly, from across the room, Mr. Zip's voice brought Bear and Peanut from their thoughts. Bear, looking at Peanut, smiled slightly, holding up his hands as if to say, *I don't know how he got there.*

"How did you do that, Mr. Zip? How'd you get there?" Peanut asked, putting into words what Bear had implied.

"You'll never know, Peanut. You'll never know. Moving on—these next three stained-glass stories tell of our history and, at the same time, our future."

"Mr. Zip, how can these windows tell about our past and our future...at the same time?"

"Well, now, hold on. This first stained glass is of the *Mayflower*." With raised eyebrows, he added, almost teasingly, "Do you notice anything different about it?"

"I'll say! That ship has red sails!" Peanut blurted out. "In all my born days, I have never seen a picture of the *Mayflower* with red sails."

Laughing, Mr. Zip asked, "Do you know who came over on the *Mayflower*?"

"Why sure. Everybody knows *that*. It was the Pilgrims."

"Yes, that's right. But *why* did they come to America?"

"To be free..." Peanut said thoughtfully, "...for

religious freedom."

At that, Bear jumped right in. "Yes, that's it, they wanted to worship God according to the Bible. They first tried to find that freedom in Holland, but didn't find what they were looking for." Shaking his head, he continued. "No sir, not at all, but *then* they heard about America. So they left Holland going back to Great Britain, finally setting sail for America on the *Mayflower*."

"Yes, that's true," said Mr. Zip. "But on that voyage, many of the Pilgrims became terribly ill and some even died. The artist who made this stained glass told me that the red sails represent the sacrifice the Pilgrims made so we could also worship God freely. You see, Peanut—our history and our future."

"I see," said Peanut, folding his arms while he thought about what Mr. Zip and Bear had just said. "So, this next stained glass is about our history and our future, too?"

"Yes. Do you know who it is?"

Peanut moved closer to inspect the window. "I think it's George Washington...but he's down on his knees, and it looks like he's praying."

"You're right, Peanut. He *is* praying."

"But I don't get it, Mr. Zip. How is this a picture about our history and our future?"

"Remember, Peanut, when we were talking about George Washington a little earlier...about how he was not only our first president, but also the Father of our Country?"

Peanut nodded. "Yessir, I remember."

"But did you know that George Washington was also a Christian?"

"No, sir. Didn't know that."

"He was, indeed. He called for his men to be good Christians, too.

"And he was often found praying by himself," Bear interjected, "especially when he knew the battle would be fierce." Then, feeling a little embarrassed, he apologized, "Oh, excuse me, Mr. Zip. Didn't mean to interrupt."

"That's okay, Bear. I get carried away, too, sometimes." Then, turning to Peanut, he said, "This stained glass reminds me of how George Washington's Christian faith was a building block for our nation."

"I don't know what you mean, Mr. Zip."

"Not only was George Washington a man of integrity and honor, but the way he lived everyday life and his faith in God inspired those around him." And then seeming to change direction, Mr. Zip asked, "Have you ever admired anyone, Peanut?"

"Why, yessir, my brother, Pocket. He's so smart, but he's fair, too."

Mr. Zip furrowed his eyebrows. "How so, Peanut?"

"Pocket does bookkeeping for the sawmill. Sometimes he finds mistakes in his calculations after paychecks have been handed out. He could hide the mistakes, but no, he always makes sure the men are paid their fair share, even when it looks bad on him. He takes responsibility, yessir, responsibility. I want to be like him, you know, always doing the right thing."

"Well, there you go. Just like you want to be like your brother, many wanted to be just like George Washington, including those who wrote the Constitution. So...the way George Washington lived his life helped to lay the foundation of our nation, giving us the basis for our future laws. You see—our history and our future."

Mr. Zip was walking over to the last window and was about to speak when Peanut let out a small gasp. "Mr. Zip, this window is so different from the others...I mean, it's still beautiful, but, it seems more...simple. There are just rays of sunlight cutting through dark clouds. I don't know why, but it somehow makes me feel...hopeful."

"That's good then. That's what the artist wanted to do, to bring hope."

"Sooo, the dark clouds are our past, our history"— and wrinkling his nose, as he was prone to do when figuring something out—"and the rays of the sun, our future?"

Mr. Zip and Bear replied at the same time, "Oh, I hope so, Peanut. I hope so."

…that "the pretzel was actually created in 610 A.D. by European monks — and the shape was meant to resemble the crossed arms of a person in prayer"[6]?

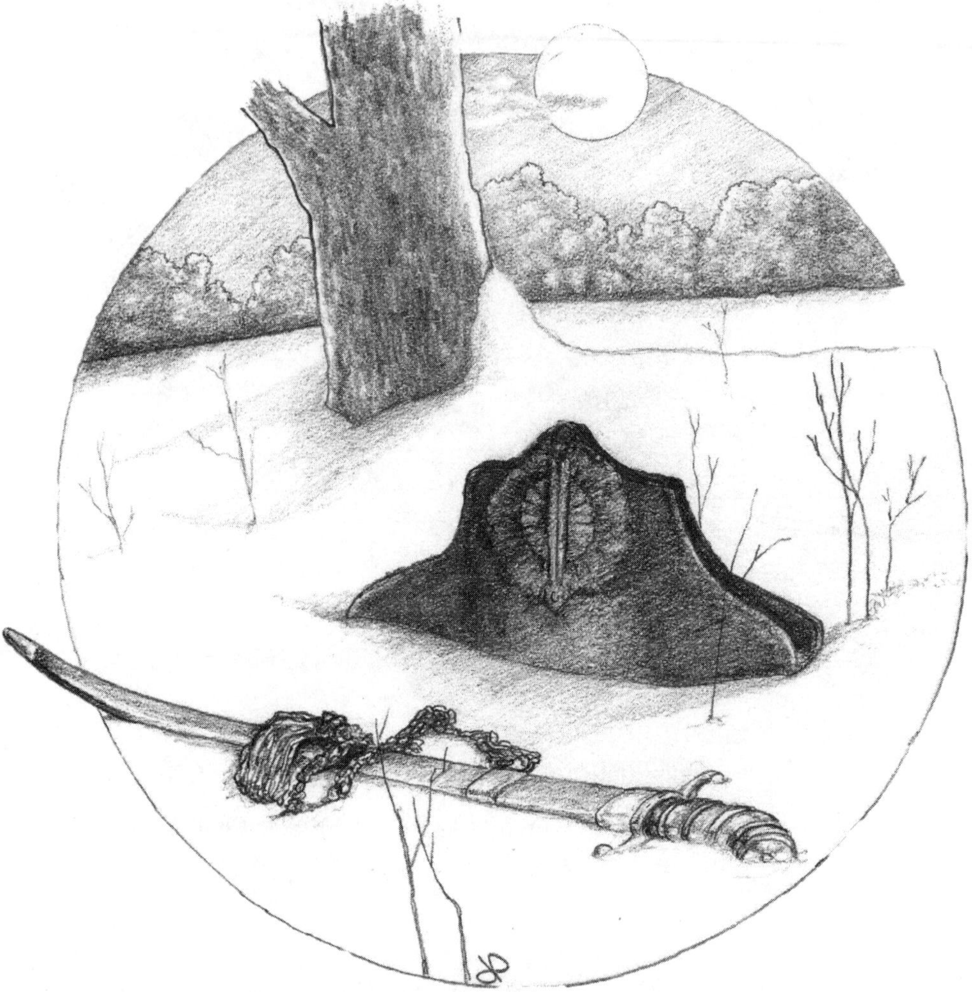

Chapter 6

A Cold and Lonely Night

S uddenly and unexpectedly, Mr. Zip walked over and jumped on the saddle. "Come on!" he said with a big smile, while tossing Bear and Peanut the tricorne hats he had grabbed when he first dashed into the room.

No longer surprised by the happenings inside The This and That Shop, Peanut joined Bear and Mr. Zip. Sitting astride the saddle, Mr. 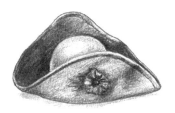 Zip placed his tricorne on top of his head. He didn't say a word, but waited as if expecting someone...or something. Peanut glanced nervously around the room, a bit afraid, but also a little curious as to what might happen next. And Bear, smiling, stood by as if he knew a secret that *he* wasn't about to tell.

Then, as gently as the sunset pales to dusk, the magnificent, light-filled room began to dim. The sunny, hot day became a cold, dark night....

Snow began to fall and, shivering, Peanut looked up. Instead of books and stained-glass windows, he saw the treetop shadows of tall pines, evergreens, and oaks, etched along a darkened skyline. The comfortable smells of well-worn leather sofas, cherry pipe tobacco, and inviting fires also began to fade, giving way to the surprisingly acrid smell that comes with falling snow on bitter winter nights.

The wind, still gusting, swirled the last of the brown, withered oak leaves to the ground, also sending the heavy clouds scudding across the sky. Gradually, the snow stopped falling. The winter moon, peeking through the clouds, glistened on the freshly fallen snow. No one moved.

Even though a thousand questions were flying through his mind and his heart was beating wildly, Peanut stood still, very still. Just when he thought he could stand it no longer, the crackling of frozen branches broke the silence. Peanut glanced in the direction of the sound.

Emerging from the edge of the woods, coming quietly through the curtain of trees into the clearing, was George Washington on his horse. Peanut's jaw dropped. Bear and Mr. Zip watched silently.

Washington reined in his horse, dismounted, and started to walk over to them. Even though Peanut was stunned speechless, he could see that General Washington looked worn and weary. Bear, who was accustomed to these adventures with Mr. Zip, was shocked at the General's appearance.

Without hesitation, Bear stepped forward and held out his arm. General Washington walked his horse over to him. Wrapping the reins loosely around Bear's arm, he allowed the end of the reins to come to rest in the huge hands.

He paused for a moment, looking gratefully into Bear's eyes, and without a word, turned and headed back to the center of the clearing.

The General had taken no more than three or four steps when, with a shuddering sigh, he sank to his knees. Taking off his hat and sword, he laid them on the ground, buried his head in his hands, and began to pray such a prayer that the brokenness of his heart could be heard in almost every word. "Dearest Lord God, God of Armies," General Washington prayed, "I beseech Thee, to interpose Thy Divine Aid as we are in crisis; to come to the aid of our country's cause, of humanity's cause, and of the world."⁷ His prayer was so passionate that Peanut's heart began to ache. And Peanut, along with Bear and Mr. Zip, dropped to his knees reverently, removing his tricorne hat.

He was listening so intently that he almost didn't hear the soft crunching of footsteps on snow, coming from the woods. Peanut looked up. In the pale moonlight, he could barely make out the figure of a man wearing a very wide-brimmed hat. The man was carrying a small lantern and was walking, in a respectful, watchful way, toward General Washington. Halting, he also knelt down.

Somewhat concerned for General Washington's safety, Peanut was about to ask who the man with the hat might be, when he felt Mr. Zip's firm, but gentle hand squeezing his shoulder. He looked up to see Mr. Zip nodding that all was well and whispering that he would explain later.

When Peanut's gaze returned to General Washington, he knew that the general had not moved, but his shoulders, which had been bent beneath his burden, had somehow lifted. His eyes open and looking toward heaven, were now filled with peace, a peace that Peanut recognized because he had seen it in his own daddy's eyes. The plaintive prayer had turned to the soft whisperings of gratitude and thanksgiving.

After what seemed like no time at all—although Peanut knew that quite some time had passed because the moon had shifted in the night sky—General Washington rose to his feet. Picking up his sword and placing his hat on his head, he walked over to Bear who handed him the reins. With a nod, General Washington led his horse to the top of a hill.

Peanut, Bear, and Mr. Zip followed. Looking down the hill, they could see the tops of hastily built log cabins, where George Washington's soldiers were sleeping. General Washington stood there for a moment. The moonlit night that had seemed to hold fear and uncertainty was now peaceful and still. And even though he couldn't tell you why, Peanut knew that everything was going to be okay.

George Washington mounted his horse and slowly moved to the edge of the forest and down the hill. When he disappeared over the crest, the moon, the outline of trees, the snow, and half-frozen mud melted into...

...the bright sunlight of a hot July day. The book-lined walls of the library began to reappear, along with the stained-glass windows and stone fireplace. The acrid smell of frozen snow had also vanished. Once again, the room was filled with the welcoming fragrance of cherry blend tobacco, worn leather sofas, and friendly fires. Peanut was about to ask if what he had just seen was real...when Bear's deep, heartfelt laugh broke the silence. "I just love coming in here!" he said, through rolling laughter that seemed to fill every corner of the room.

Peanut just stood there. He could not *believe* that Bear was laughing after all they had seen and heard.

Mr. Zip's lively chuckle, joining Bear's deep bass rumble, started to resemble a musical duet. Peanut, who didn't understand what was going on, first began to grin, and then for reasons unbeknownst even to himself, joined in the contagious sound.

As the "music" slowly subsided, Mr. Zip was finally able to speak. "Now, Bear, why did you come to see me this morning?"

Bear, who was still chuckling, but doing his best to stop, said, "Why, Mr. Zip, I was bringing you my newest flavor of pretzel—salty cinnamon." Pulling out of his pocket something smooshed that could have been a pretzel at one time, Bear gave a good-natured shrug accompanied by an apologetic grin. "Oh, well, think I'd better run back to my pretzel stand and get you a fresh one." With that, Bear moving as hurriedly as a man who lumbers like a bear could move, made his way to the front and, with the tinkling of bells, went out the swinging doors of The This and That Shop.

"Come here, Peanut." Sitting down and settling back into the sofa as if he were going to be there for a while, Mr. Zip pulled out his pipe and began tapping the bowl on the bottom of his shoe to dislodge any leftover tobacco. Peanut sat beside him, watching as Mr. Zip carefully unrolled a bag of tobacco, stuffing pinches of it into the bowl of the pipe. Lighting the pipe and taking a puff, a restful calm descended on the room. Even though Peanut still wanted to know if what had just happened really *did* happen, he, too, was content to wait....

"You know, Peanut," Mr. Zip began between puffs, "do you remember how I told you that The Capital Z is a shop filled with this and that?"

"Yessir, Mr. Zip."

"And you remember that many things in The This and That Shop are reminders of our history, of who we are and where we came from?"

"Yessir, Mr. Zip."

"Well, what happened with George Washington just now was one of those reminders, a reminder of what really did happen long ago."

"But it seemed so *real*, Mr. Zip."

Mr. Zip leaned toward Peanut, coming so close that he was almost eye to eye and nose to nose with the young boy. "It truly was a *real* reminder, Peanut, a *real* reminder."

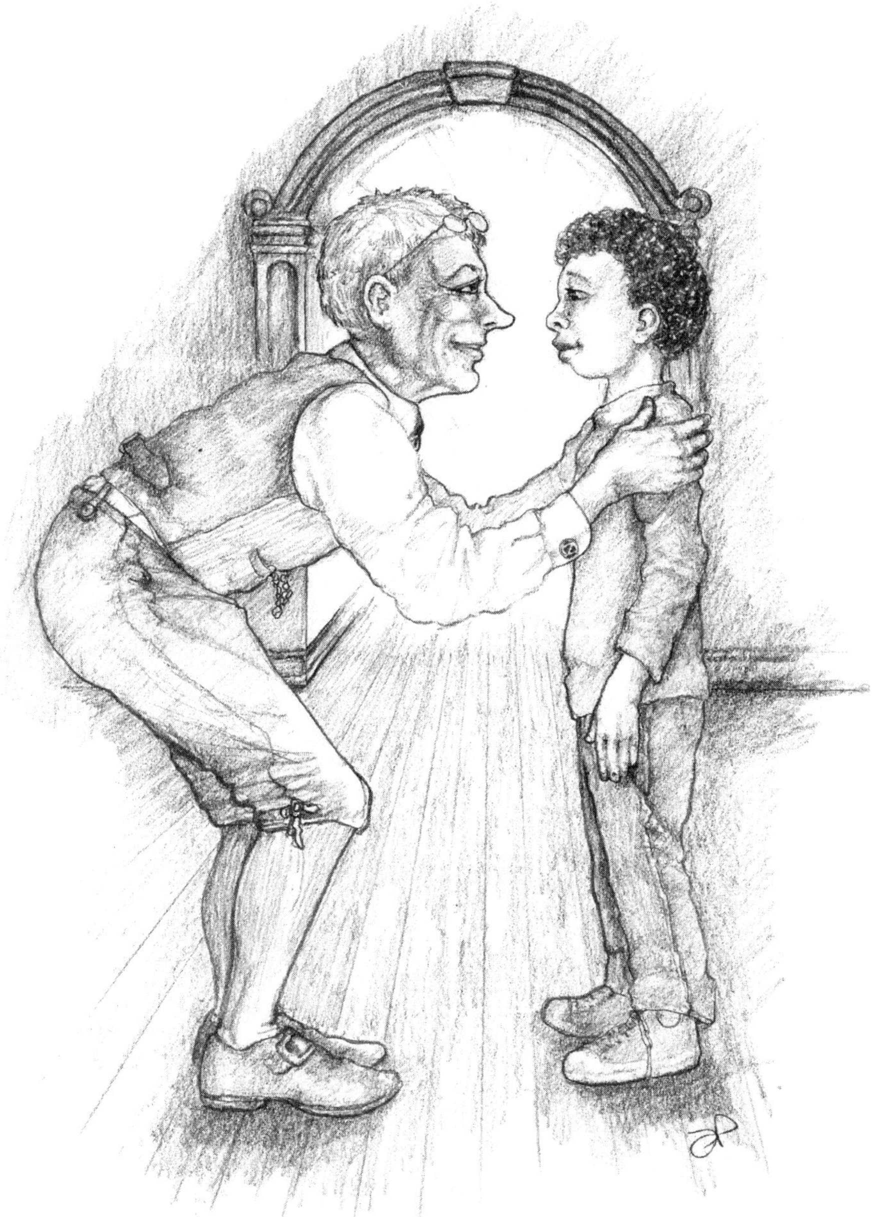

...that the cabins that George Washington's men stayed in at Valley Forge were actually hastily built by the men themselves?

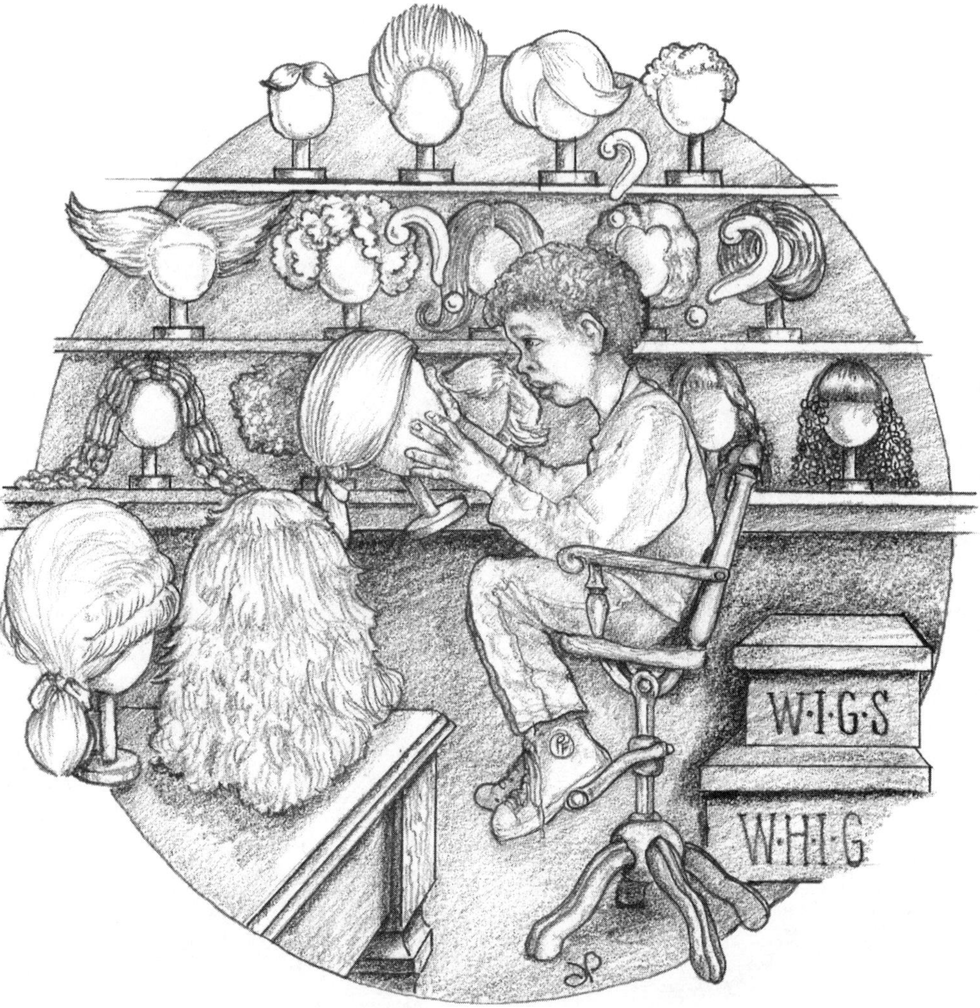
W·I·G·S
W·H·I·G

Chapter 7

A W-I-G???

Peanut wrinkled his nose and crossed his arms in a "hrumph." He had just opened his mouth to object when Mr. Zip spoke first. "Peanut, do you remember the gentleman wearing the big-brimmed hat who came from the edge of the woods when we were in prayer with George Washington?"

"Yessir..."

"Have you ever heard of Quakers, Peanut?"

"No," Peanut replied thoughtfully. "No, sir, I don't believe I have. Who are they, or what are they?"

"Quakers, also called the Religious Society of Friends, are Christian believers much like the Pilgrims. The man you saw coming out of the woods as George Washington was praying was a Quaker."

"But *how* do you know *that,* Mr. Zip?"

"The big-brimmed hat he was wearing was part of the customary dress for Quakers in George Washington's day. More importantly, though, this Quaker is known in history as Isaac Potts, the man who overheard George Washington's prayer that cold evening. Did you know that what he heard actually changed his life in a significant way?"

"No, but how do you know *that?* Mr. Zip, how do you know everything?"

"Why, there was an eyewitness account, of course! Nathaniel Randolph Snowden, an ordained Presbyterian minister, who graduated from Princeton, knew Quaker Potts. Mr. Potts gave him a firsthand account of what happened that evening. He told Snowden that he saw General Washington alone in the woods, praying. I think Snowden's exact words were: 'I got it from himself, myself.' Here, let me read it to you. It's in my encyclopedia."

Mr. Zip, untangling his wiry arms and legs, jumped up from the sofa and zipped, as his name would suggest, over to the bookshelf. "Let me see, where is it? Ah, yes, here it is." Bringing the volume to the sofa and sitting back down, he began to read aloud:

> "I knew personally the celebrated Quaker Potts who saw Gen'l Washington alone in the woods at prayer. I got it from himself, myself."[8]

Peering over his spectacles at Peanut, Mr. Zip continued reading:

> "Weems mentioned it in his history of Washington, but I got it from the man myself, as follows: "I was riding with him (Mr. Potts) in Montgomery County, Penn'a near to the Valley Forge, where the army lay during the war of ye Revolution. Mr. Potts was a Senator in our State & a Whig. I told him I was agreeably

surprised to find him a friend to his country as the Quakers were mostly Tories. He said, 'It was so and I was a rank Tory once, for I never believed that America c'd [could] proceed against Great Britain whose fleets and armies covered the land and ocean, but something very extraordinary converted me to the Good Faith!"

"What was that," I inquired?

'Do you see that woods, & that plain. It was about a quarter of a mile off from the place we were riding, as it happened.' 'There,' said he, 'laid the army of Washington. It was a most distressing time of ye war, and all were for giving up the Ship but that great and good man. In that woods pointing to a close in view, I heard a plaintive sound as, of a man at prayer. I tied my horse to a sapling & went quietly into the woods & to my astonishment I saw the great George Washington on his knees alone, with his sword on one side and his cocked hat on the other. He was at Prayer to the God of the

Armies, beseeching to interpose with his Divine aid, as it was ye Crisis, & the cause of the country, of humanity & of the world.

'Such a prayer I never heard from the lips of man. I left him alone praying.

'I went home & told my wife. I saw a sight and heard today what I never saw or heard before, and just related to her what I had seen & heard & observed. We never thought a man c'd be a soldier & a Christian, but if there is one in the world, it is Washington. She also was astonished. We thought it was the cause of God, & America could prevail.' "He then to me put out his right hand & said 'I turned right about and became a Whig.'"[9]

"A wig?" Peanut screwed up his nose again. "He became a *wig,* like what people wear on their heads?"

Mr. Zip laughed right out loud, so hard, he could barely catch his breath. "No, Peanut, not a wig you wear on your head, but a W-H-I-G—a political party in George Washington's day. Whew!" Mr. Zip straightened his vest, regaining his composure.

"Oh, you mean like the Republicans and the Democrats?"

"Yes, but let's back up and look at American history. Before the Revolutionary War, there were thirteen American colonies that were under British rule. King George, the King of England at that time, began to impose terrible and unfair taxes on the people living in the thirteen colonies. Those unfair taxes caused some people in the colonies to want to rebel, to break away from the rule of such a king.

They became known as the Whigs. People in the colonies who wanted to remain under the rule of the king were called Tories. Quaker Potts was a Tory—that is, until he heard George Washington pray. His prayer touched Quaker Potts so deeply that Mr. Potts changed allegiances and supported America's rebellion. Why, Quaker Potts actually ended up *helping* George Washington!"

"How'd he do that?"

"Quaker Potts saw that General Washington's men were hungry. He also noticed that their clothes were worn and ragged, barely able to protect them from the December cold. After he heard George Washington's prayer, he offered the general food and clothing for his men."

"Well, I never," said Peanut. "George Washington's prayer did change Quaker Potts's heart. I wonder if I would be brave enough or have enough faith to pray like George Washington prayed."

"How do you mean, Peanut?"

"Well...I mean if I was George Washington, I probably would have sent my men to hunt, or maybe even to neighbors in the surrounding countryside and ask for food. But George Washington...why, he just went straight to God. When Quaker Potts heard that prayer, he gave George Washington's men the food and clothing they needed so badly. That's somethin', Mr. Zip. That's just really somethin'!"

Mr. Zip waited a moment while Peanut thought about this mighty big idea before asking, "Do you know what the Bible says about this very thing? The Bible says, 'God honors those who honor Him.'[10] So, in other words, God took care of George Washington and his men because Washington trusted Him."

…that the name *Whig* first appeared in Scotland?
It came about during the Wars of the Three Kingdoms
(1639-1651) and was used to describe Scots who fought
against the British.[11]

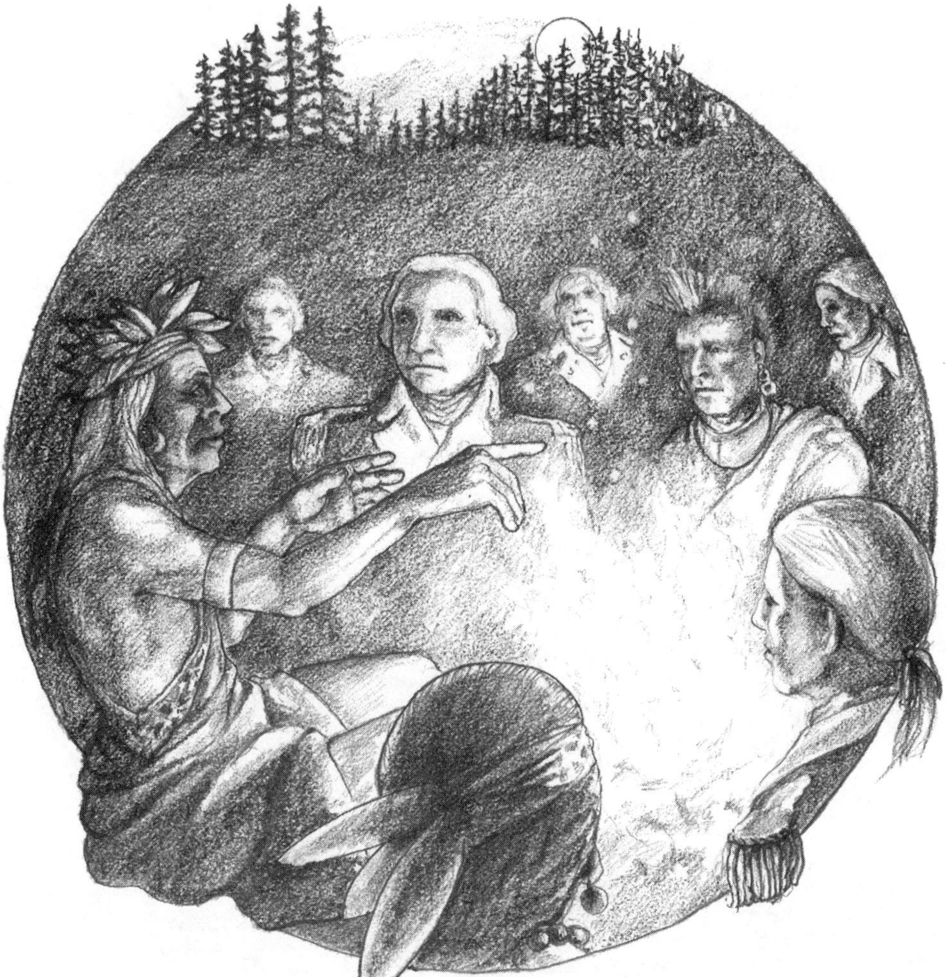

Chapter 8

An Indian Chief and
a Tall Daring Warrior

D o you want to hear another true story about George Washington, Peanut? You might not believe me. Some would call it a humdinger!"

Peanut laughed. "Yessir, I'd like that. All of your stories are real exciting, Mr. Zip. I just don't know where they will take me next."

"Well, then." Mr. Zip hopped up and stood by the sofa. Stooping down, his arms and hands out in front like he was about to paint a landscape with words, his eyes widened with excitement. "Bullets were flying everywhere...just EVERYWHERE."

Suddenly a bullet went whizzing past Peanut. Peung! And again. Peung, peung, peung! He quickly crouched down, covering his head with his arms. When he did, he saw that he was wearing a red coat...and that he and Mr. Zip were once again outside.

"What's going on?" Peanut yelled.

"Come on, Peanut!" Grabbing Peanut's hand, Mr. Zip began to run across an open field. It was not just any field, but one where a terrible

battle was raging—and they were right in the thick of it! Peanut, pulled along by Mr. Zip, was crouching and running and at the same time trying to cover his head with his arms. Peung! Another bullet zipped past Peanut's head. Peung, peung, peung!

"Mr. Zip!" Peanut, overcome with fear, yelled wildly, barely recognizing the sound of his own voice. At that moment, Mr. Zip pulled Peanut to the ground, the two of them landing just inside the edge of the woods behind a log. Peanut lay there, face down, arms covering his head, as if that would protect him from the bullets that kept flying past him. All he could hear were those bullets...well, those bullets and his heart, which was beating so wildly and so loudly, he thought it was going to beat right on out of his chest!

Not daring to lift his head—not even an inch—he whispered as loud as he could, "Mr. Zip."

"Peanut, look!"

Peeking out of one tightly closed eye and turning his head just a little, Peanut could see Mr. Zip leaning on his elbows, watching what was happening on the battlefield. "Mr. Zip, get down!" he said, frantically tugging at his elbow.

"It's okay, Peanut. They're not shooting at us. We're safe, but look who they ARE shooting at." Mr. Zip pointed toward the battlefield.

Barely poking his head up, almost like a turtle would poke his head out of his shell, Peanut looked again. Squinting through twigs and leaves that had become tangled in his hair, he could see the figure of a man on a white horse, madly galloping back and forth and shouting to his men.

"What have you gotten me into this

time, Mr. Zip? Whoever is shooting at the man on the white horse could start shooting at me, at us, any minute!" Peanut suddenly stopped. "Mr. Zip, is that who I think it is? Is that George Washington?"

"Shhhh," whispered Mr. Zip, "look at the woods to your left and just behind us."

At first, Peanut could not see anything but trees, bushes, and lots of tangled underbrush. Then he saw it, a slight puff of white smoke. Squinting so he could see better, he thought he could make out the shadowy silhouette of an Indian, and then another, and another. They seemed to rise up like ghostly figures, shoot their rifles, then disappear back into the brush.

The fighting on the battlefield grew more fierce, the sound of it like a growling thunderstorm building with terrible intensity.

"Mr. Zip, they're all shooting at George Washington." At that very moment, Washington's horse fell to the ground, trapping him underneath! Peanut jumped up. "Oh no, he's trapped! We've got to help him."

Just then, George Washington freed himself, leaping onto another horse whose rider had been shot.

"Did you see that, Mr. Zip?" but as Peanut said those words, the woods they were hiding in and the battle they were watching disappeared.

Peanut found himself and Mr. Zip sitting with Washington and a company of his officers at an Indian council fire. Peanut looked incredulously at Mr. Zip who very calmly nodded and pointed for Peanut to look directly across the fire. Sitting there was a very old—to Peanut, incredibly ancient—distinguished-looking Indian chief, surrounded by his braves.

The old chief began to speak."Lishke hatak api humma inmimko apelichi..."[12]

"What did he say, Mr. Zip? What did he say?"

At that moment, a young brave began to translate:

"I am a chief and ruler over my tribes. My influence extends to the waters of the great lakes and to the far blue mountains. I have traveled a long and weary path that I might see the young warrior of the great battle. It was on the day when the white man's blood mixed with the streams of our forests that I first beheld this chief [Washington].

I called to my young men and said, "Mark yon tall and daring warrior? He is not of the red-coat tribe - he hath an Indian's wisdom and his warriors fight as we do - himself alone exposed. Quick, let your aim be certain, and he dies."

Our rifles were leveled, rifles which, but for you, knew not how to miss - 'twas all in vain, a mightier power far than we shielded you.

Seeing you were under the special guardianship of the Great Spirit, we immediately ceased to fire at you. I am old and shall soon be gathered to the great council fire of my fathers in the land of the shades, but ere I go, there is something bids me speak in the voice of prophecy:

Listen, The Great Spirit protects the man [pointing at Washington] and guides his destinies - he will become the chief of nations, and a

106

*people yet unborn will hail him as the founder
of a mighty empire. I am come to pay homage to
the man who is the particular favorite of Heaven,
who can never die in battle.*"[13]

With those words, Peanut found himself back in The
Capital Z, with Mr. Zip sitting beside him on the now familiar
sofa. "Peanut, did you know that George Washington's coat
was actually hit four times during that battle, but with none
of the bullets striking him?"[14]

Shaking his head in disbelief, Peanut wrinkled
his nose. "No, I didn't know that. But, Mr. Zip, we both
smell like campfire smoke. This time, it really *had* to have
happened, right?"

Winking, Mr. Zip replied, "A splendid reminder,
don't you think? Yes, a splendid reminder."

Did You Know

...that after the battle, Washington, who was a colonel at that time, wrote a letter to his brother, saying, *"Dear Jack: As I have heard since my arrival...a circumstantial acct. of my death and dying speech, I take this early opportunity of contradicting both, and of assuring you that I now exist and appear in the land of the living by the miraculous care of Providence..."*[15]?

Chapter 9

The *Real* Tale of the Cherry Tree

D id George Washington really sit at a council fire across from an Indian chief? That reminder of what we just saw, did that really happen to George Washington, Mr. Zip?"

"Yes, Peanut. As a matter of fact, it did. Why do you ask?"

"Well, because I've never been taught that in school before. Why is that?" Peanut scrunched up his face, puzzling over this question.

"Peanut, you have just opened the proverbial can of worms, yes sir, a can of worms, to be sure."

"You don't have to explain that to me, Mr. Zip," Peanut said, shaking his head. "I *know* what 'opening a can of worms' means. Problems, problems, problems, ummm, ummm, ummm."

Mr. Zip smiled. "Over the years, things having to do with God, Divine Intervention, have slowly been removed from our textbooks. It has happened gradually. One minute it's there, and seemingly, the next mimute—poof!—it's gone. It's really an insidious thing."

"That doesn't seem right." And then holding up one

hand, Peanut said, "Waaait a minute. Stop right there, Mr. Zip. What does *in-sid-i-ous* mean?"

"*Insidious* means 'to proceed in a gradual, subtle way, but with harmful effects,'" Mr. Zip explained.

"Ooo, I get it. It's like when a snake is slithering toward you through the grass. One minute it's not there and the next, it's crawling by your foot!"

Mr. Zip let out a belly laugh. "I couldn't have said it better myself, Peanut. Yes, like a slithering snake." And then, more thoughtfully, he added, "But you know, isn't that what happens in our own lives?"

"I don't understand what you mean at all, Mr. Zip."

"Well, let's look at choosing to tell the truth or choosing to lie. Have you ever told a lie, Peanut?"

"Aw, Mr. Zip, everyone's told a lie," Peanut said, fidgeting with the laces on his tennis shoe. Then, mustering his courage, he looked Mr. Zip directly in the eye. "Yessir, I *have* told a lie."

"You want to tell me about it?"

"It was nothing, really. 'Least not at first....'" He twisted his lips in a funny little pucker as if he had just popped ten sweet-and-sour candies into his mouth all at once. "I told Mama I was late coming home from school one day because I had stopped to talk to the teacher after school." Rushing on, almost defensively, he said, "And that really was the truth, too! I *meant* to talk to the teacher, but I saw some boys playing baseball and thought to myself that one time at bat would be okay...and I would talk to the teacher after I finished playing." Shuffling his feet some more, he dropped his voice. "The trouble was, Mr. Zip, the teacher left before I got to talk to her. When I got home, I told Mama I was late because I stayed after school to talk to the teacher. And then it happened."

"What was that, Peanut?"

"The interrrogution...the interrogala..."

"The interrogation?" Mr. Zip kindly interjected.

"Yes, that's it, interrogation. I knew something was wrong when all the questions started."

"What kind of questions?" Mr. Zip asked, imagining the scene, while trying to hide a smile.

"You know, Mr. Zip. Like, 'Why did your teacher want to see you?' 'What did she say to you?' and 'What did you say back?' And then the worst one of all: 'Well, Peanut, why in the world would your teacher call me and ask me to remind you to stop by the classroom TOMORROW?' Oh, man," Peanut said shaking his head. "It was hot coals of fire."

"Hot coals of fire?" Mr. Zip almost laughed out loud again, but then saw the serious look in Peanut's eyes.

"Yessir, it's like being too close to hot coals of fire. I started sweating something fierce. I kept trying to come up with a good excuse, but I was stumbling so bad on my words, I just stopped talking." Peanut's face took on the same blank expression he probably had when he was facing his mama.

Peanut groaned. "I knew my goose was cooked! I

should have just told the truth. It really was no big deal, but boy, when I lied to my mama, *that* turned into a really big deal."

"Hmmm. So...would it be safe to say that it's better to tell the truth?"

"Yessir, Mr. Zip," Peanut said mournfully, nodding his head. "When I first told that lie to my mama, it seemed like it was hidden, kind of like that snake in the grass. But when I was found out, it was worse than finding the snake between my feet. It was almost as bad as being *bitten* by that snake, Mr. Zip! Lying is not worth it."

"And how could *that* be, Peanut?"

"Well, I didn't get to play ball for two weeks, TWO WHOLE WEEKS. That hurt really bad, Mr. Zip, but you know what hurt even worse than that?"

"What? Do tell."

"My stomach. The minute I told my mama that I had stayed after school to talk to the teacher, my stomach balled up in a knot. And with each question my mama asked, the knot got tighter. It hurt so *baaad*. I knew what I was doing was wrong, but I just couldn't seem to stop."

"Hmm, I know how that is. I'm guessing you'll think twice about telling a lie from now on?"

Peanut nodded, his sincerely polite, deeply brown eyes wider than ever. "Yessir, I won't go down that road again, but if I accidentally fall into or start to tell one, I'm going to sit on my lips." Then adding as an aside, "That's an expression my mama uses."

Mr. Zip cocked his head and raised his eyebrows.

"Well, if you sit on your lips, you can't exactly talk, can you?" Then Peanut, with his lips closed, demonstrated: "Mmh...Ip...mn...uh..un...r...an...mh?"

Laughing, Mr. Zip said, "I get your point...Peanut, remember the cherry tree story you were asking me about earlier today?"

"The one where George Washington didn't lie," Peanut said in resignation. "I know what you're going to say, Mr. Zip...."

The tone of Peanut's voice told Mr. Zip that he really didn't want to hear one more word about how wonderful George Washington was.

"Now, hold on a minute...I think you might like the *real* story of George Washington and the cherry tree, as told by Reverend Mason Locke Weems."

"Reverend Mason Locke Reems? Who is he?"

"Weems," corrected Mr. Zip. "Or, as most folks called him, *Parson* Weems. Parson Weems lived from 1759 to 1825 and wrote the first bestseller on Washington, *Life and Memorable Actions of George Washington*, 9th edition. In that book is the most famous of all his stories— the 'cherry tree' story. I have that book."

Abruptly, Mr. Zip jumped up and ran to fetch it from the shelf. Settling back into the sofa, he said, "As Parson Weems tells it, George was about six years old when he became the proud owner of a hatchet. He was extremely fond of that hatchet, and he was also equally fond of chopping everything in sight. One day he came upon a beautiful English cherry tree that grew in his mother's garden. Well, young George just couldn't resist trying the edge of his hatchet on the tree."

"'Trying the edge of the hatchet'?"

"Yes, 'trying the edge of the hatchet' means that while you don't chop down the tree, you cut into the bark, injuring the tree so badly it won't recover. Well, the next morning, young George's father found the much-injured cherry tree, which by the way, happened to be one of his favorites."

Peanut's eyes were as round as saucers as he whispered, "I bet *I* know what happened next." And in that very instant, Peanut found himself in the room with George Washington's dad. Mr. Zip had disappeared, but Peanut could still hear him telling the story that he was witnessing firsthand. Quickly, Peanut ducked behind a desk, biting his lip in anticipation of the trouble young George might be in.

> *"Would someone please tell me what happened to my beautiful cherry tree? And if you cannot do that, please find me that mischievous Master George. I need to speak with him."*
>
> *Presently George and his hatchet made their appearance.*
>
> *"Yes, sir, Father. You wanted to see me?"*
>
> *"George," said his father, "do you know who killed that beautiful little cherry tree in yonder garden?"*
>
> *George, staggering under this tough question for a moment but quickly recovering, said, "I can't tell a lie, Pa; you know I can't tell a*

lie. I did cut it with my hatchet."

"Run to my arms, you dearest boy," cried his father in transport, run to my arms; glad am I, George, that you killed my tree, for you have paid me for it a thousand fold. Such an act of heroism in my son is worth more than a thousand trees, though blossomed with silver and their fruits of purest gold."[16]

Mr. Zip clapped the book closed and with that, Peanut found himself back in the Capital Z.

"It really *did* happen, Mr. Zip. I saw it with my own two eyes!"

"We don't know for sure, Peanut, but neither George Washington himself nor the people who knew him, nor Parson Weems ever disputed this story. What intrigues me even more, though, is George Washington's father's response to his favorite tree being destroyed. Peanut, his dad was actually glad! So…what do you think about *that?"*

"Well," said Peanut, thinking it over, "maybe, just maybe his dad wasn't so glad he killed the tree, but *maybe* he was glad that his boy told the truth."

"Exactly. You're onto something, Peanut!" said Mr. Zip. "And that is the *greater* lesson that comes from the 'cherry tree' story."

"Bigger than not telling a lie?" Peanut asked, his sincerely polite, deeply brown eyes now growing enormous.

"Now, don't get me wrong, Peanut. Telling the truth is of the utmost importance, but first, let me ask you a question. Wouldn't you agree that we all do things we wish we could undo, or that if we *just* had a second chance, we could go back and do it right the first time?"

"Oh, Mr. Zip, I sure do. I know what I'd redo. I'd redo the day before yesterday. I didn't *mean* for Lovie Dovie to get hurt. I didn't mean for any of it to happen. What am I going to do? My daddy's not ever going to trust me again."

Walking over, Mr. Zip put his arm around Peanut. "Oh, it's not that bad. What did we just find out about the cherry tree story? George Washington's dad didn't get mad at him, did he?"

"Noooo," said Peanut woefully, "but that's because George Washington did the right thing by telling the truth."

"Very true. But didn't George Washington do wrong in the first place in killing the tree—a tree that everyone knew his dad loved?"

"I suppose so," Peanut said, feeling a tiny surge of hope.

"And don't you think his father was glad because George Washington owned up to what he had done...you know, took responsibility for his actions?"

Peanut's heart gave a little leap. "You mean I could do that, too? I could own up to my dad? I could make it right?"

Mr. Zip stood there for a moment studying Peanut and then without warning, he took off. "Follow me!"

Peanut raced after him. When he reached the front of the shop, Mr. Zip was already standing there, holding something tightly in his closed hand. "Peanut, I have something for you."

"What is it, Mr. Zip?" Peanut twisted his head sideways to see if he could possibly get a peek at what was inside Mr. Zip's fist.

He didn't have to wait too long because Mr. Zip opened his hand. "This was a pin that supporters of George Washington wore for the first presidential inauguration in 1789. These very first political pins, made of brass, were more like buttons and were sewn on clothing. Instead of photos, these buttons had slogans printed on them. Photos weren't used until Abraham Lincoln ran for president."

"What does this one say, Mr. Zip?"

"See for yourself, Peanut."

Peering into Mr. Zip's hand, Peanut saw that in the center of the button were the initials "GW." Then, aloud, he read slowly as he made out the words: "'Long live the president.' Wow, this is neat, Mr. Zip."

"Why, here you are, Peanut. Go ahead. Take it. It's yours."

"Really, Mr. Zip? You want me to have this button?"

"Yes, indeed," Mr. Zip said with a big smile. Then more seriously, "Peanut, this really was one of George Washington's inaugural buttons. So take really good care of it. Put it in your pocket and always carry it with you. It will be *your* reminder, a reminder of who you are and where you came from. It is a reminder to you of who you are when you succeed and who you are, even when you fail. Everyone fails at one time or another. But, remember, it's what you do when you fail that counts."

As if suddenly remembering something, Peanut said excitedly, "Mr. Zip, I've got to go!" Running toward the front door, Peanut stopped abruptly, ran back, and hugged Mr. Zip around his waist. "Thank you, Mr. Zip. Thank you." And because what he was feeling was much too big for words, all he could finally say was a heartfelt, "You just don't know...."

With that, he hurried toward the door. He was about to grab for the handle when suddenly the double doors were flung open, and a young girl about the same age as Peanut burst through, slamming into Peanut, just about knocking him down.

"Oh, sorry, Lucy Jane," Peanut apologized. And then to Mr. Zip, "See ya."

With that, he turned again to leave, but not before hearing Lucy Jane—that is, the one and only Miss Lucy

Jane Pennywhistle—say, "Hmmph! Watch out where you're going, Peanut Johnson!" And then, spotting Mr. Zip, she said, "Mr. Zip, you're not going to *believe* what *my mother* bought me!"

As the doors of The Capital Z swung shut, what Lucy Jane Pennywhistle was saying to Mr. Zip was lost. But that didn't matter because Peanut Johnson was already at the end of the street. He *had* to get home. He had to see his mama and dad...'specially his dad.

...that there were over 25 designs of George Washington's inaugural buttons that people could choose from?

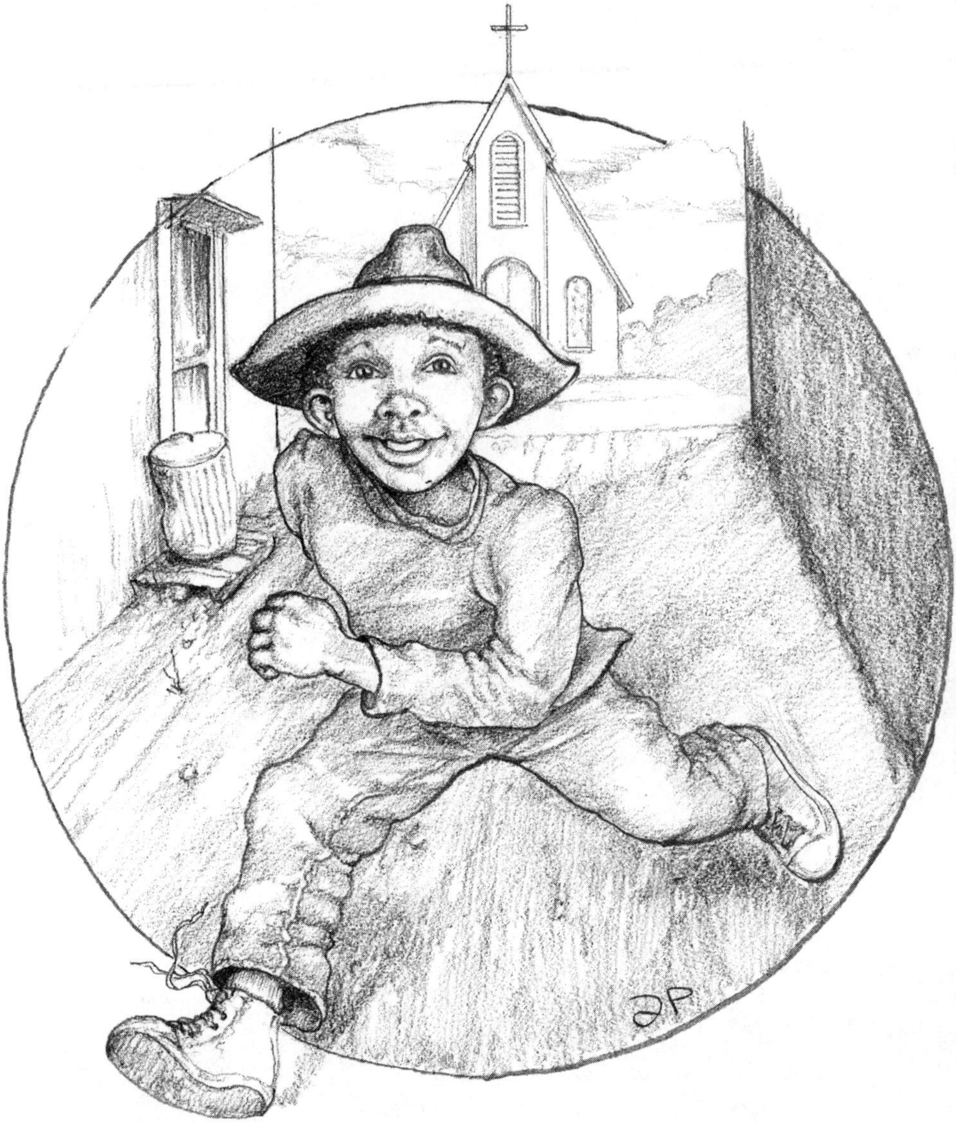

Chapter 10

A Change of Heart

In no time at all, Peanut burst through his own front door. The first person he saw was his sister Secret. Breathless from running *all* the way from town and barely able to get the words out, he gasped, "Where are they, Secret?"

His sister, who had almost fallen asleep on the sofa as she was listening to music on this hot July day, jumped up. "Peanut! Slow down. You just about made me leap out of my skin. Where is *who*? Is everything okay?"

"Yeah," Peanut said, still panting, "everything's okay. I've just got to find Mama and Dad. Where are they?"

"Oh, Peanut," Secret said with the tiniest bit of exasperation, "you scared me half to death. They're out in the garden." With that, she plopped back down, settling into the sofa cushions…and into the music of Brahms.

Turning on his heel and running out the back door and headlong into the garden, Peanut came to a sudden halt, partly because he didn't want to trample the garden and partly because he didn't know what he was going to say when he got there.

Placing his nervous hands in his pockets, he slowly

walked toward his parents who were picking tomatoes. They were laughing and talking quietly together, so they didn't hear Peanut approaching, didn't really know he was there until he cleared his throat. "Uh, hi, Mama. Hi, Dad."

His dad was the first to reply. "Well, hi there, son. What have you been up to today?"

Before he could answer, his mama looked up, her soft eyes full of love for him. "Hello, Peanut. How are you?"

"I'm okay. How's Lovie Dovie?"

"She's fine, son. She's taking a nap right now," said his mama.

"That's good. That's real good." Peanut stood there for a few seconds, the warm summer breeze gently rustling the leaves of the old oak tree.

After a minute, his dad spoke up. "Peanut, son, you got something on your mind?"

"Yessir. Yessir, I do. You see, I went walking to town today, and I found this place called The Capital Z, and I met a man there named Mr. Zip."

"You met Mr. Zip?" Early Johnson asked with a slight smile that he seemed to be trying to hide.

"Yessir, yessir, I did. I did meet Mr. Zip. Why, Daddy? Do you know him?"

"You could say that I do, but it's been quite a few years since I *met* him and a long time since I've *seen* him." Early Johnson's expression took on a faraway look, and the years seemed to almost melt away from his gentle but careworn face as he thought of the time that *he* had met

Mr. Zip. Then suddenly turning to Peanut's mama, Early Johnson said, "Hon, let's quit gardening for the day. I want to talk with Peanut."

Wisely, knowing that her husband needed some time alone with their son, Kat Johnson smiled sweetly and started back toward the house. When she reached Peanut, she stopped and gave him a quick kiss on the top of his head. "You men don't be too long now. Supper will be ready soon."

"Come, son," Mr. Johnson said quietly. "Let's go sit under the oak and watch the sun set."

"Okay, Dad." Peanut followed his dad to the old oak tree. The sun had just dipped toward the horizon, and the summer sky was filled with all the soft pinks and purples that come at the end of a summer day. The crickets, welcoming nightfall, had begun their evening song, and, in the distance, was the first faint glimmer of fireflies. Peanut and his dad sat there for a few moments without saying a word.

At last, Early Johnson broke the silence. "Tell me about Mr. Zip, son. Tell me what you saw at The This and That Shop."

"Well, Dad," Peanut began with some reluctance, still holding onto what had happened the day before yesterday, and wondering if his dad was thinking about it, too, "The This and That Shop is really something. I mean it seems to have everything." And then, almost seeming to forget his troubles, he blurted out, "I saw Great-Great-Great-Great-Uncle Milkweed's Kentucky rifle, and George Washington's sword, and the most beautiful stained glass you'd ever want to see, and..."

Smiling, his dad held up his hand. "Whoa, wait a minute, Peanut. So, The This and That Shop hasn't changed too much since I was there...a long time ago."

"You saw all this, too?"

"Yes, son. I got to see it, too." Early Johnson laughed. Then, growing more serious, he said, "But what I really want to know is not what you saw with your eyes, but what you saw with your heart."

At that moment, Peanut's hands, still in his pockets, stumbled across the George Washington button that Mr. Zip had given him. All of a sudden, he knew what his dad was truly asking him.

Sitting up straight and looking his daddy in the eye, Peanut said, "Dad, I truly want to ask your forgiveness for what happened with Lovie Dovie the day before the Fourth of July. I really blew it. You gave me a responsibility and, instead of doing what I knew I was supposed to do, I put what *I* wanted first. I was real selfish, Dad, and because of my selfishness, everyone suffered, 'specially Lovie Dovie. I know I can never make it up to everyone—to Lovie Dovie, the family, to Mama and you—but, Dad, all I can tell you is that from now on, I'm your man. You can always count on me...."

As Peanut's words trailed off, the last remnants of the day disappeared into the summer night, the first evening star twinkling at the edge of the sky. Peanut waited. He knew his dad no longer seemed to be upset about the day before yesterday, and deep in his heart, he knew his dad loved him, but still...

Then, Early Johnson, his velvety voice a little husky with emotion, said, "Come here, son." Putting his arms around Peanut and holding him close, for just a bit, this big, gentle man understood that at the tender age of twelve, his son had just taken his first steps from boyhood into those of a trustworthy young man. Letting go, so that he and Peanut were eye to eye, Early smiled.

What Peanut saw, he didn't expect, for his dad's eyes were filled with pride and respect. Peanut suddenly knew that something big, something significant had happened and that he was somehow different in his heart. He wasn't quite sure why, or how, but he knew deep inside, everything was going to be okay.

Looking at his dad with his deeply brown, sincerely polite, and *now* merry, mischievous eyes, Peanut grinned. "Let's go inside, Dad. Let's not keep Mama waiting. Besides, I'm hungry!"

Notes

Chapter 1

1. "Hunters of Kentucky," was a song written in 1821 by Samuel Woodworth, celebrating the role of Kentucky sharpshooters in the Battle of New Orleans. One fourth of General Andrew Jackson's army was made up of Kentucky militiamen.

♫

"Hunters of Kentucky"

Ye gentlemen and ladies fair, who grace this famous city,
Just listen, if you've time to spare, while I rehearse a ditty;
And for the opportunity conceive yourselves quite lucky,
For 'tis not often that you see a hunter from Kentucky.
Oh, Kentucky, the hunters of Kentucky!

We are a hardy, free-born race, each man to fear a stranger;
Whate'er the game, we join in chase, despising toil and danger.
And if a daring foe annoys, whate'er his strength and forces,
We'll show him that Kentucky boys Are alligator horses.
Oh Kentucky, the hunters of Kentucky!

I s'pose you've read it in the prints, how Packenham attempted
To make old Hickory Jackson wince, but soon his scheme repented;
For we, with rifles ready cock'd, thought such occasion lucky,
And soon around the gen'ral flock'd, the hunters of Kentucky.
Oh, Kentucky, the hunters of Kentucky!

You've heard, I s'pose, how New-Orleans is fam'd for wealth and
*   beauty—*
There's girls of ev'ry hue, it seems, from snowy white to sooty.
So Packenham he made his brags, if he in fight was lucky,
He'd have their girls and cotton bags, in spite of old Kentucky.
Oh, Kentucky, the hunters of Kentucky.

But Jackson he was wide awake, and was not scar'd at trifles,
For well he knew what aim we take, with our Kentucky rifles:
So he led us down by Cypress swamp, the ground was low and
    mucky;
There stood John Bull in martial pomp, and here was old Kentucky.
Oh, Kentucky, the hunters of Kentucky!

A bank was raised to hide our breast, not that we thought of dying,
But then we always like to rest unless the game is flying;
Behind it stood our little force, none wished it to be greater,
For every man was half a horse and half an alligator.
Oh, Kentucky, the hunters of Kentucky!

They did not let our patience tire, before they showed their faces—
We did not choose to waist our fire, So snugly kept our places;
But when so near to see them wink, we thought it time to stop 'em,
And 'twould have done you good I think to see Kentuckians drop 'em.
Oh, Kentucky, the hunters of Kentucky!

They found at last 'twas vain to fight, where lead was all their booty,
And so they wisely took to flight, and left us all our beauty,
And now if danger e'er annoys, remember what our trade is,
Just send for us Kentucky boys, and we'll protect your ladies.
Oh, Kentucky, the hunters of Kentucky!

Source: *The Hunters of Kentucky* (New York: Andrews, Printer, 38 Chatham St., N. Y. [n. d.])

Chapter 2

2.   www.thehermitage.com/jackson-family/andrew-jackson/military-man

Chapter 3

3.   www.srcalifornia.com/washbio.htm
4.   Mark A. Beliles and Stephen K. McDowell, America's Providential History (Charlottesville, VA: Providence Foundation, 1989), 160-161.

Chapter 4

5. "Model T," A & E Networks, accessed May 29, 2015, http://www. history.com/topics/model-t

Chapter 5

6. Read more about pretzels: http://www.nnydailynews.com/life-style/ eats/pretzel-twistedhistory-article-1.1543835#ixzz3B5BP5fAq

Chapter 6

7. The actual quotation was a paraphrase from Quaker Potts, as recorded in Diary and Remembrances of Reverend Nathanael Randolph Snowden, owned by the Historical Society of Pennsylvania. ushistory.org/valleyforge/Washington/prayer/html

Chapter 7

8. Ibid.
9. Ibid.
10. I Samuel 2:30
11. en.wikipedia.org/wiki/Whigs_(British_political_party)

Chapter 8

12. We don't know exactly the native American language spoken by the Indian chief, but Choctaw was chosen because it is considered to be a basic native American language.
13. Peter Lillback, George Washington's Sacred Fire (Bryn Mawr, PA: Providence Forum Press, 2001. Printed in the United States of America by Dickinson Press, 2006—First Edition), 164-165
14. Ibid., 161.
15. Ibid.

Chapter 9

16. George Washington's father, as quoted in *George Washington's Sacred Fire* by Peter Lillback with Jerry Newcombe. George Washington's Sacred Fire (Bryn Mawr, Pennsylvania: Providence Forum Press, 2006), 693.

Kimberly Bryant-Palmer is a native of Panama City, Florida, but has lived in many parts of the United States. With a double major in Music and Biology from Mary Washington University, she has worked in cancer research and now enjoys a whole new world—writing music and books with her husband.

Jerry Palmer graduated from Harding University in Searcy, Arkansas, in 1978. He has worked as a scenic artist in film and television, and as Art Director for the Nashville Network in Nashville, Tennessee. He now resides in Franklin, Tennessee, with his wife, Kimberly, their two crazy dogs, one sane cat, and three opinionated horses.

Coming Soon!

Mr. Zip and The Capital Z~
Lucy Jane Pennywhistle Comes Home